DOMINOES AT THE CROSSROADS

Dominoes
at the
Crossroads

STORIES

Kaie Kellough

ESPLANADE BOOKS

THE FICTION IMPRINT AT VÉHICULE PRESS

ESPLANADE BOOKS IS THE FICTION IMPRINT AT VÉHICULE PRESS

Published with the generous assistance of the Canada Council for the Arts, the Canada Book Fund of the Department of Canadian Heritage, and the Société de développement des entreprises culturelles du Québec (SODEC).

Canada Council   Conseil des arts
for the Arts   du Canada

This is a work of fiction. Any resemblance to people or events is coincidental and unintended by the author.

Esplanade Books editor: Dimitri Nasrallah
Cover design: David Drummond
Typeset in Minion and Filosofia
Printed by Marquis Printing Inc.

LIBRARY AND ARCHIVES CANADA CATALOGUING IN PUBLICATION

Title: Dominoes at the crossroads : stories / Kaie Kellough.

Names: Kellough, Kaie, 1975- author.

Identifiers: Canadiana (print) 20190234709 | Canadiana (ebook) 20190234717 | ISBN 9781550655315 (softcover) ISBN 9781550655360 (EPUB)

Classification: LCC PS8571.E58643 D64 2020 | DDC C813/.6—DC23

Published by Véhicule Press, Montréal, Québec, Canada

Distribution by LitDistCo
www.litdistco.ca
Printed in Canada.

Contents

Contents

Maître des trois chemins, tu as en face de toi un homme
qui a beaucoup marché
Depuis Elam. Depuis Akkad. Depuis Sumer.
Maître des trois chemins, tu as en face de toi un homme
qui a beaucoup porté
Depuis Elam. Depuis Akkad. Depuis Sumer.
J'ai porté le corps du commandant. J'ai porté le chemin
de fer du commandant. J'ai porté la locomotive du
commandant, le coton du commandant. J'ai porté sur
ma tête laineuse qui se passe si bien de coussinet Dieu, la
machine, la route

   –Aimé Césaire

Simply, a Caribbean story could not really be told
without reference to servants. Don't forget that, after
all, as a black person, I descend from the slaves, and the
slaves were always silent, forced to be silent. They knew
they were the real masters of the island.

   –Maryse Condé

La question ordinaire et extraordinaire[1]

From the *Canadian Journal of Caribbean and Diaspora Studies*, Issue 208.4.4, "Changes."

First published as "Notes toward a keynote address, on the 475th anniversary of the city of Milieu."

We gratefully acknowledge the *Black Electronic Milieu Ontological Review* for hosting and organizing the 475th anniversary event, and for granting us permission to republish this address.

1. Thanks and Opening Remarks

I WOULD LIKE TO THANK everyone for attending tonight. This event, with its holographic re-creation of Rockhead's Paradise,[2] inside of which we are seated right now, and its holographic performance by Oscar Peterson, giant of 20th century jazz, is a fitting way to celebrate the 475th anniversary of one of the oldest cities in North America, a city that is always reimagining itself. I am grateful to be in Milieu, once known as Montréal, and once—and still—as Tiohtiá:ke.

I would like to thank the editors of the *Black Electronic Milieu Ontological Review* (BEMOR) for their commitment to thinking about Black history and the city, and for their generous invitation to speak at the launch of this issue. The question we will be examining today is one of belonging in the city of Montréal. The Black presence on these shores dates back to the origins of New France.[3] Black belonging, which is arguably a dominant feature of today's city, has appeared at other times as extraordinary, as contested, and even as undesired.

Fortuitously, this event coincides with the 50th anniversary of the death of my great great grandfather, Kaie Kellough, whose name a few of you will know. Kaie was a 21st century author who wrote several books before the gradual collapse of publishing in the first half of that century. Today we experience tension between the older digital technologies and ID (Instant Dissemination), whereas during his time the digital world was challenging the older world of curated publishing, copyright, physical objects that one had to purchase to access "content."

Kellough's content, much like mine today, often looked at place and identity. In the city of his day, he saw the various social, cultural, and economic positions navigated by Black citizens. He also saw the way Black histories were constructed as minor narratives, and as narratives that ran counter to official Québec histories. This allowed for the suppression and minimization of the contributions of Black Quebeckers to Québec culture, and for an erasure of their historical presence. Let us imagine for a moment that we are in the Milieu—then Montréal—of 150 years ago.

In the late 1970s the English were in decline, and the French were gradually establishing their political dominance in Québec. The English continued to coexist, and they maintained their privilege (a telling descriptor in Kellough's time) but they had relinquished their hegemony over the future. A new city was emerging from the ground, or from the street, up, as Kellough often emphasized in his fiction. The street, meaning public space in the city, was important to him as physical, and not as theoretical or virtual space. It was in the street, and not in a parliamentary bill, or a panel among culturati on Radio-Canada,[4] where Montréal's identity emerged.

In Kellough's early writing the street often meant downtown, but over time its definition broadened to encompass less central urban neighborhoods and even the near suburbs. Those areas were home to immigrant populations who visibly informed the diversity of the island, but who were relegated to the off-center boroughs, because housing was cheaper, and cultural communities, which could provide a source of support for newcomers, were established. The central and southern parts of the island were becoming wealthy enclaves, in a phenomenon opposite that of White Flight,[5] another 20th century demographic trend. Kellough noted that in the early 2020s, this movement of wealth, both domestic and international, toward the center, and the movement of people seeking affordable housing away from the center, was evidence of Montréal becoming less oriented toward any traditional hub called "downtown." The various boroughs were establishing themselves as unique, affordable, self-sufficient economic and cultural hubs. This trend was hastened by two factors.

The first, in 2017, was the creation of the Royalmount urban megaproject. Initially a luxury development, it was locally maligned, and then rejected by the municipal administration. It languished, incomplete, as partners withdrew. It was eventually subsumed by a culturally mixed urban planning committee, called the Sepia Future Seers. The SFS proposed a development based on an amalgam of digital models of urban neighborhoods in New York, Montréal, Rome, Barcelona, Medellín, Rio, Berlin, and Beirut. The project would feature affordable rental units alongside properties for purchase, of varying values, and intricate commercial zoning to accommodate variety among businesses. Independent ethnic grocers would sit next to established café chains, fripperies next to upscale furniture stores, artisanal boutiques next to corporate franchises. This was jokingly labeled the "cheek by jowl" approach, and despite a media establishment that lambasted the idea as naïve, the idea transformed the derelict megaproject into a populous city center. Its residents successfully lobbied the city for a westward expansion of the public transit system, and Royalmount emerged as a rival to the traditional downtown core. The success of Royalmount shifted Montréal's demographic balance in one remarkable way. Media opposition to the project made it very difficult for the SFS developers to find tenants and on-spec buyers. The SFS decided to advertise exclusively in communities with high concentrations of immigrants. Royalmount was branded as a new beginning, whose prosperity would be powered by its diversity. Despite criticism that this branding was an attempt to monetize identity, the brand succeeded. The second factor was the climate crisis of 2040, to which we shall return.

ii. Historical Overview of Milieu

Slide: Periods and Names of the City

[Note: This slide is to stay up for the remainder of the presentation.]

Indigenous Period: Tiohtiá:ke (Ongoing)
Colonial Period: Ville-Marie (1642-1705)
Old Port Period: Montréal (1705-1976)
Urban Period: Montréal (1976-2055)
Climate Crisis Period: Lamontagne (2055-2143)
Post-Climate Crisis Period: Milieu (2143-present)

[Reference the slide.]

THE HISTORY OF MILIEU can be divided into six distinct periods, four of which are identified by a change of name that coincided with a significant event. Although distinct, the periods still overlap. The Indigenous and Colonial periods, for instance, are ongoing in the Post-Climate Crisis Period. It is also argued that the Climate Crisis began well before it was officially declared. While these timelines can and should shift, the main point is that the city's changing circumstances have informed how the city identifies and how it promotes itself.

Each version of the city contains the previous. This is difficult to grasp in the context of the Colonial Period, because its proponents attempted to wipe out much that had previously existed on this territory. The same is true for the Climate Crisis Period. While there is debate about how deliberate the crisis was, the crisis did submerge sections of the city. These sections are unlivable; they are visited by explorers, adventurers, and marine research expeditions. Both periods share the experience of deliberate destruction, of loss. Expansion distinguishes the other periods. The Old Port Period expanded on the Colonial. The Urban Period began in the Old Port and expanded northward.

In spite of the centuries that have passed, the shifting geography of the city, and its increasing and declining size, two figures from the overlap between the Colonial and Old Port periods resonate through all subsequent Montréal history. Those two were captured in this excerpt from an unfinished work of short fiction by Kellough:

My name is Mathieu Léveillé. I was a slave in Martinique. I was transported to Québec as an executioner, and I was responsible for the torture and execution of the slave Marie-Joseph Angélique. Before I had any such duties to perform, I rode in a canoe with Angélique, from Québec to the port, along the St-Charles River.

It was June, and daylight prevailed into evening. Angélique sat across from me, bound. She seemed to stare through me, as if her gaze were light itself. What could she see in me? All I wanted was to fill myself with rum, enough to blur the river, the canoe, the authorities, the entire colony. I was appointed to extract her confession, which would come with the application of les brodequins. If she survived, she would have only fire to anticipate, the same fire that the Conseil Supérieur found her guilty of lighting, and which destroyed the port.

I thought of plunging into the river, diving to the bottom and drowning there. I have tried to drown before. I don't know how to swim. I have always been sick. When I was in Martinique I became so ill I couldn't work, but everyone must work, and I became the instrument of the sickness that is bondage. I was forced to perform a repellent job. My troubles are nothing in her eyes. My life is ash when illuminated by hers.

Once we reached the port, whose ground was blackened by fire, we took Angélique to prison, where I fastened les brodequins tight to her bare shins, inserted the wedges, and lifted the hammer. I was doing what I was forced to do. It was declared in her sentence, it was declared that she should be tortured until she confessed to having deliberately lit the fire, and once confessed, she would be placed in a wagon on her shattered knees, with a torch in her hand, and the wagon would be driven through the streets of the port, and she would declare her guilt then beg forgiveness, and do this again and again until she had been seen and judged by all. She would then be hanged facing the charred ruins of the home of the widow de Francheville, and finally her body would be burned and her ashes scattered.

Angélique does not see me. Or if she does, she doesn't show it. I am nobody to her. The June sun beads on her forehead and she is sitting upright, with the chains around her wrists and ankles. Her chin is tilted up, ever so slightly, and her nostrils are flared, as if in defiance or—[6]

Kellough does not explicitly write about a future Montréal, but in this excerpt, as in other works, his future city is implied. It exists in the cities of the past and of the present, and it is up to us to read this. He has elsewhere[7] stated that he is not interested in futurisms, which for him involve projecting an aestheticized vision of a city that stands at the center of its culture. Rather, he wishes to examine the various urban properties that may one day emerge to shape the future. What are those properties? In Kellough's writing, for instance in his novel *Accordéon*,[8] they are the diversity that exists at street level in the city of Montréal, which is encountered every day in the public sphere, but is suppressed in official accounts and in official hierarchies. Kellough notes, in his personal correspondence,[9] that the 375th celebrations of the "founding" of Montréal were marked by an advertisement that was filmed in various locations throughout the city, and that did not feature a single Montréaler of color. Yet, when Kellough visits those same locales on any given weekday, he is himself a person of color occupying public space, and he encounters others like himself. The advertisement and its perpetrators were part of an effort to theorize people of color out of belonging and participation, perhaps out of the future, perhaps even out of existence. The quotidian reality, as well as the historical reality, is different.

In the above excerpt, the city itself is a charred, blackened ruin that will need to be rebuilt, but first it will need to be reimagined. Instead of focusing on the loss of property and the devastation caused by the fire, which was lit in 1734, he focuses on the common ancestry, class, and the improbable, tragic rapport between the two enslaved people in the canoe.

And it is precisely those children of (im)migrants from the Antilles, from Africa, and from many other regions, who will arise not only to populate but to seize and shape the future. But the point is finer: those children have already populated, seized, and begun shaping. The future is already in their hands and minds. Today's metropolis, Milieu, already existed in the pre-Climate Crisis Montréal that Kellough knew, but what this excerpt suggests, is that it also existed in a much older version of the city, one that was burned down by a woman of African descent, one that had to be radically reimagined. Kellough notes this in *Dominoes at the Crossroads*,[10] where he also tells us that this need for radical reimagining was as necessary in the 1700s as it was in the 1900s. To what degree is it necessary now? Milieu is one cohesive island civilization, but it is also one in which there no longer exists a dominant ethnic group. No group can claim a 50% or greater share of the population.

III. The 2040 Climate Crisis

In Eastern Canada, the years following 2016 dawned with heightened anxiety, a political turn to the right, an emphasis on an overt language of ethno-nationalism in federal and provincial politics, plus a rise in the presence and number of right-wing hate groups. Some groups took vigilante measures, armed themselves, and attempted to patrol the border to prevent what they saw as illegal immigration.[11] This turn to the right was interrupted by the climate crisis of 2040.

As 2040 approached, the polar ice caps had undergone extensive melt, and water levels rose to the critical point. The Saint Lawrence River gradually overwhelmed its banks. Water seeped into businesses and residences along the southwestern-most part of the Island. Parts of Nun's Island, Île Ste-Hélène, Île Notre-Dame, and Longueuil found themselves uninhabitable. Residents abandoned Habitat 67 and the Cité du Havre area, and received no compensation for the loss of their exclusive homes.

Twenty years earlier, Montréal's southwest had been transformed into a luxury riverfront borough, with condominium towers erected along its banks, and developers refashioning the late 19th century industrial buildings into exclusive loft housing. Severe flooding rendered the southwest uninhabitable. The Old Port was submerged.

Insurance companies, fearing being bankrupted by claims, redrew the maps of areas they considered insurable. In this way they managed to avoid large payouts, but many formerly wealthy residents of Montréal became a displaced class, and were referred to as "domestic migrants", in Milieu. Naturally this did not happen to everyone, and in spite of whatever lingering historical resentments, the residents of the northern boroughs opened their homes to their displaced neighbors in a display of civic generosity that the media celebrated. The northern boroughs doubled in population, the ethnic mix of these neighborhoods was transformed, and the economic balance that had once governed Montréal shifted in the new city of Milieu. The advent of the name change is a topic for another paper,[12] but it is worth noting that much of the downtown core was abandoned, and the center of the city was erased. The name change was an ironic reflection of there being no center, or of every part of the city in fact becoming its own center.

One of the radical changes that the city underwent, one that Kellough could not have foreseen, was the sudden spike in the value of homes that were further up the island. These areas, many of them lower income and home to (im)migrants and communities of color, became the most valuable areas on the island, and the resulting balance of financial power shifted into Haitian, North African, and Latin-American hands. Formerly wealthy descendants of Wolfe and Montcalm found themselves applying to Haitian landlords for apartments to rent in St-Michel, and many of them, left destitute after the flooding, failed their credit verifications.

IV. Futures

KELLOUGH'S NOTION of the future is informed by the city's Black history. The future is encoded in the past, and in certain events that decide our lives for us. One such event was the 1734 burning of the city, attributed to the enslaved woman Marie-Joseph Angélique. Born into bondage in Portugal, Angélique is an atypical progenitor. Even though she was a mother of three children, including twins, she was an arsonist and a murderess. Her act, one that prominent 20th and 21st century scholars, including Dr. Afua Cooper, believed to be deliberate, was one of massive destruction. The fire that she lit, by placing hot coals in the roof beams of the de Francheville home on the rue St-Paul, then blowing on them, destroyed a large portion of the port of Montréal, which was later known as the Old Port, and is now known as Pirates' Town, an underwater amusement park. She destroyed the city, but her act forced the citizens to reimagine and rebuild. That history-altering act was carried out by a member of a population that was consistently marginalized. It is telling that today, with much of Old Montréal submerged, her story is prominent, and she is venerated as an ancestor of Milieu.[13]

¹ *La question ordinaire et extraordinaire*: The question, which was a torture in the Middle-Ages in France, was a way of discovering the truth. It was often combined with a water treatment, or with *les brodequins*, the boots. The ordinary question involved the application of the torture, and the extraordinary question saw its intensification. In 1734 in the port of Montréal, the enslaved woman Marie-Joseph Angélique was submitted to the question. The boots were applied to her legs by formerly enslaved Martiniquais Mathieu Léveillé (1709-1743), who was brought to New France to serve as Angélique's executioner. She confessed to setting her mistress's house on fire, but even when the extraordinary question was applied, she refused to reveal her accomplice, rumored to have been her (White) lover, Claude Thibault, who fled New France following the arson.

² *Rockhead's Paradise*: Famed jazz venue in the Little Burgundy District of Montréal named after its proprietor, Jamaican-born Rufus Rockhead.

³ *Mathieu Da Costa* (1589-1619) was a translator, and the first free Black person to land in Canada. He traveled with Samuel de Champlain.

⁴ Radio-Canada was the Francophone side of Canada's national broadcaster. The broadcaster's public funding was cut, and it was dismantled in the first half of the 21ˢᵗ century. Its reestablishment was undertaken by Antillean Marxists, and it became the familiar *Voix Libre International*.

⁵ *White Flight*: A phenomenon that originated in the United States in the 1950s, when people of various European ancestries migrated en masse from racially mixed urban regions to more racially homogeneous suburban or exurban regions.

⁶ Excerpt from an unfinished story begun by Kellough in 2017-18. Concordia University Records Management and Archives (Kell-1074-02-128).

[7] Kellough, Kaie. "Montréal: Slavery, Revolt, and the Future." Interview with Dr. Nalini Mohabir and Dr. Ronald Cummings, in *Canadian Journal of Caribbean and Diaspora Studies* 48.4.4 (2017): p. 516-539.

[8] Kellough, Kaie. *Accordéon.* ARP Books (2016).

[9] The correspondence in question was drawn from Kellough's email. Concordia University Records Management and Archives (Kell-1074-02-146).

[10] Kellough, Kaie. *Dominoes at the Crossroads.* Véhicule Press (2019), p. 19.

[11] Through 2017/18, in response to a tightening of US immigration policy, thousands of undocumented migrants crossed into Québec on foot. 4,000 slept on military cots at the Olympic Stadium. Kellough references these migrants in *Magnetic Equator*, and predicts that they will one day "inherit the city." On reaching the border, some migrants were met by armed vigilantes, affiliates of a group of disenfranchised Whites calling themselves La Meute (The Wolfpack), who wore shirts printed with the image of a wolf.

[12] *Name Change*: The first Muslim mayor of Milieu (the city was then known as Lamontagne), Djamila Aboutair (2100-), was responsible for the name change. Aboutair was a descendent of the French and Algerian philosopher Jacques Derrida. Aboutair noted, on several occasions, that the name Milieu was chosen in reference to Derrida's work.

[13] In "Montréal: Slavery, Revolt, and the Future," Kellough, Cummings, and Mohabir note that the fiercest opponents of imperialism and slavery in the Caribbean, those who led rebellions, who marooned, who advocated tirelessly for freedom, are venerated as national heroes in their respective countries. They argue that those same honors should be paid to Marie-Joseph Angélique.

Porcelain Nubians

SATURDAYS MY GRANDFATHER would take me to the St-Michel Flea Market. Though I haven't been there in decades, I remember its mingled odor of dust, petroleum jelly, sweat, mold, and even after smoking was banned indoors, how its air was weighted with old tobacco. I imagined that its walls breathed nicotine and tar, and the building that housed the market, built in the 1940s or 50s like so much of St-Michel, just like the house we lived in, had asbestos in the walls and was one immense, ailing lung. The merchants, many old, bent Québécois men and women—some with drooping yellowed moustaches like retired Prussian generals—would take every opportunity to slip outside and smoke a cigarette, and the smoke would blow inside with the winter air when the door opened. The merchants always showed a mixture of suspicion and warmth when my grandfather greeted them. They showed respect because he was old and his manners were impeccable, but they withheld some basic intimacy because of his distance from them. To them, no matter how long he lived here, he was from *ailleurs*, and his accent always confirmed this.

St-Michel itself, even though it was on the metro line, the blue line, the narrow blue streak over the mountain and into the east, was like a little bustling elsewhere within the city. It was an elsewhere where Arab men squatted on the sidewalk outside a café, holding saucers on which they perched tiny cups of espresso, while smoking cigarettes and watching the shoppers on Jean-Talon Street. It was an elsewhere where short Central American women balanced groceries on their heads. It was zigzagging power lines and housing jumbled without a thought toward zoning or consistency. It was a concrete high-rise next to a single-level shoebox. It was Haitian teenagers laughing on the sidewalk and Italian seniors staring at them out of lace curtained windows. It was a sloping floor and no soundproofing, it was the lingering question of the rent cheque, and it was the unceasing bustle to and from metro St-Michel, the queues of Black and Brown people on St-Michel Boulevard waiting for another bus heading farther east. It was the Jehovah's Witnesses in the metro, in their orthopedic shoes and black stockings, holding *Awake!* and *Watchtower*, with their coats buttoned against each blast of cold air when the doors swung open, it was sometimes the extremes of being saved, or of being ensnared. It was the bustle and the pressure that rose from the Crémazie expressway in the mornings and rattled the entire borough awake. It seemed like elsewhere, but it was here, the easternmost stop on the blue line, tucked in next to Villeray, whose property values were rising.

My grandfather was always on the lookout for two things: antique table radios and landscape paintings. He had assembled a collection of old radios in the basement, with names like Grundig, Brando, and Silvertone, radios he'd restored. I used to turn out the lights and tune them all to the static between channels, then pretend I was either adrift on a raft on the ocean or shuttling through the cosmos. He also loved generic landscapes, with tall pines set back from winding streams, mountains in the distance, or lakes bordered by rocky shores atop which evergreens narrowed to the sky. He dusted and repainted the frames and hung the landscapes throughout the house. I would stare into them, into the peacefulness and space that they offered, and I always thought of how different they were from the busy neighborhood framed by our windows. In those paintings I saw distances that I wanted to enter to leave the neighborhood behind. At night I might dream myself standing in a clearing that I had observed in a painting, but I would be a different version of myself, always exhausted from having just run, always out of breath, always glancing over my shoulder worried that the mastiffs might be after me, and men a short distance behind them, yet staring ahead toward the river and the skirts of the evergreens that swayed in the night wind, and I knew that only a little farther and I might enter the future, where I could stop running. I would wake up in my room in St-Michel, listening to the voices and cars out the window, and the smell of the flea market hovering in the room.

My grandfather smelled much sweeter than the *marché*. There was something elemental about its smell, just like there was about him. He had always been present, as far as I, and even my parents, could remember. He remembered *Ayiti* in ways that they couldn't. He remembered a more hopeful and peaceful time, before Montréal loomed on the earth's clouded curve. He also remembered his parents, who had told him about their parents, whose own parents might have stood with Dessalines atop a citadel, biting down on a lead musket ball to stave off hunger and thirst, as they prepared to repel a French ambush, and their parents before them who might have been bound in iron and shipped across from Ghana, or Benin.

After my grandfather died, I stayed away from the *Marché aux Puces*. It reminded me of an older St-Michel, one that I didn't miss, one that didn't have 400,000-dollar condominiums being built, one in which the modest single family houses along 21st, 22nd, 23rd avenue weren't being bought by young couples, their interiors painted white, their linoleum replaced with cool tile or floating laminate, and high wooden fences erected around their backyards. In my remembered St-Michel, bidding wars weren't erupting over triplexes, tenants weren't being renovicted, and duplexes weren't being converted into townhouses. They were leaking, growing mold, as their landlords did little for their monthly cheques. As the neighborhood makeover progressed it appeared inevitable, as if there had never been a doubt that someday St-Michel would take off. It was decried as gentrification. Tenant advocacy groups were convened and people spoke out in the local papers. I didn't care. I was relieved to see the old neighborhood change.

My grandfather used to say that nothing is inevitable until it happens. I wondered about the inevitable things he saw, like the rise and fall of dictators or the flight and eventual landing of families on other sides of an ocean, or the shift of one language into another, the new one still retaining inflections of the old, such as the curling of a W around the edges of an R, the new shapes a tongue can never quite form. These things are bigger than us, and some are so vast that they sweep nations, or generations into that disordered library called history.

The only thing my grandfather framed and hung that wasn't a landscape was a short article he clipped from the *Globe and Mail.* I don't know how he came across the article because it was in English, which he hardly spoke, but there it was, and after he died it wound up in a box jumbled among his landscapes. I took it. The article was about an auction held at the Ritz-Carlton in the downtown's Golden Square Mile. The Montréal Ritz was the original, the first one in the world to bear the Ritz-Carlton name, and apparently that was worth conserving. It was 2008, the Ritz's elegance had faded enough that 100 million dollars in updates were planned. But before it was to be renovated, it would hold an auction. The article quoted one of the Ritz managers, discussing the items up for auction: genuine silver serving platters, crystal wineglasses, tablecloths, curtains, other Ritz memorabilia that didn't seem like it would be worth much, but then I thought of the flea market and the old adage about trash and treasure. The interview noted, curiously:

According to auctioneer Iégor de Saint Hippolyte of the Iégor Auction House, the pieces involved in the auction have more sentimental interest than value as antiques, except for a pair of statues of Black Nubian slaves, made in Venice between

1850 and 1880, that flanked the hotel's original elevator in 1912. They fetched $15,000 on Wednesday night.

An ice bucket with the Ritz logo went for $150, a wooden desk for $1,000 and a gilded mirror from the restaurant sold for $800.

None of the hotel's lobby furniture or art was on offer.

Silver-haired Louise Leclerc said she could not imagine summer in Montreal without lunches in the garden with her life-long friends.

–Heather Sokoloff, Montréal,
Special to the *Globe and Mail*, June 27th, 2008

The word "fetched" stuck with me. The slaves fetched the money, and after all of the years during which they had been attentive to the guests and the décor of the Ritz, they were sold, and they were required to fetch a large sum for others, and their fetching was noted with approval. Perhaps that was a sign of social progress, that the value they fetched was noted in a national newspaper. Whose 15,000 dollars had those slaves fetched? Where were they now, and into whose collection were they going?

The article was not accompanied by a photo of the Nubian figures, and I wondered whether the writer was using that ethnicity accurately. How would she, or the auctioneer, know that the figures were Nubians? Had they asked the figures where they were from? And if they had been in North America, via Venice, since the 1850s, might they not identify more strongly with the Black cultures of North America? I was shocked that the Ritz-Carlton had continued to practice slavery into the 21st century. It hadn't attempted to conceal this. It hadn't attempted to, say, make the figures invisible by relegating them to the bowels of the hotel, or to washing dishes in the rear of the kitchen. During working hours they were visible. They stood by the elevators and perhaps each wore a red fez cocked just so, with black skin gleaming beneath, and black tight curls close cut, and they may have stood on sizeable blocks of—ceramic?—and their hands held up large planters in which the Ritz had planted dwarf palms. Or, perhaps they each leaned back on either side of the elevators and held out bamboo fans to cool the weary tourists. As the figures cooled the tourists, they completed the image of old-world ease, and they turned time backward, toward a past in which a body might belong to another.

After hours, when the guests stopped coming and going, and the bellboys stood outside smoking on Sherbrooke Street, the Nubian figures put down their fans, or the dwarf palms whose fronds they peered between, and strolled through the lobby with its marble floor and wood paneling. Their feet, accustomed to standing on stone, eased into the carpet in the empty dining room. They sank into lavishly upholstered chairs in the rear, in darkness, with only the lights of Sherbrooke Street reflected in the windows, and they shared a spliff.

"There are no more adventures left for people like us. Our time is passed, even though it continues."

"The past continuous is a verb tense that describes actions that began in the past and that are continuing now. I suppose a person contemplates life in the past continuous."

"I think that's the only tense for the contemplation of a life."

"If so, then we carry the past into the present, and it stays relevant."

"I don't know. I feel we've reached a stationary point, whereas we used to move from city to city, we used to be coveted, now we're tucked in a corner of the hotel, and we've been here since 1912."

"Yes, things used to move faster, and while we were considered servants, decorative pieces, there was always prestige. Now it seems that we're afterthoughts."

"Afterthoughts is a euphemism. I think you mean relics."

"Relic: A surviving memorial of something past."

"Yes. I can stomach being a relic without being subjected to ridicule. We're an embarrassment—even to White people. When they see us they cringe, yet they don't have any idea where we've been."

"I think they know where we've been, but they don't think anything of it."

"They don't think."

"They think, but they don't think about us."

"The looks we get from the Black and Brown people who stay here are no better."

"The ones who work here, at least, show us some respect."

"Pity or respect?"

"Do you remember when we first landed in Venice?"

I moved out of St-Michel in my twenties, into a triplex my grandfather owned. He had the foresight to buy in the

1980s, a building built in the same year the Ritz-Carlton was established, in 1912. It had dark wood paneling, plaster moldings and high ceilings. The floorboards were narrow and long, stained a lustrous amber. The foundation was stone and mortar, solid, not the poured concrete that later became standard. The neighborhood was not prestigious when he bought, but he loved the building, he was proud to own it, and he kept it up. When he died he left it to me. Suddenly I was no longer a tenant, but instead the undeserving owner and landlord of my building. He left my parents a larger one, a five-plex built in the same era.

A wave of real estate activity washed over the Plateau before any other borough, and once it receded, the value of the triplex, which had a sizeable backyard and boasted 1,400 square-foot apartments, each with a large rear terrace, had inflated to almost a million dollars. When my parents died, I inherited their home in St-Michel. As their only child, I also inherited my grandparents' home in St-Michel, which they had previously inherited and rented out, and the five-plex. The two houses were entirely paid off, as were both tenant buildings, and I was suddenly, through no effort or interest of my own, a minor real estate investor. I enrolled in a course with Re/Max to become a licensed broker.

I decided to keep the tenant buildings, update them, and transform the basements, which were being used by the tenants as storage space, into additional rental units. I increased the rent to the maximum market value. As for the houses, I decided to sell. I tore up carpet, re-finished hardwood, painted the interiors powder white, and listed them both. I donated old family possessions to merchants at the St-Michel Flea Market. My grandfather's table radios and landscapes returned to the dust and clutter from which they had been rescued. They lost their meanings. The spaces that the landscapes had opened up in our home were now closed, compressed with the rest of the neighborhood. Dining cabinets and dressers now belonged to noone, they became idle material. Sets of matching dishes were stacked among other sets of matching dishes. Cheap silverware returned to its box and was shelved with other sets of cheap silverware.

The Re/Max signs bearing my face went up, and within a month both houses sold above the asking price. Both sold to young French families. Both families installed chicken coops and planted vegetable gardens in the back-yards. I retained all but 2% of the commissions.

Those homes were my final tie to the old neighborhood, the immigrant neighborhood, the point of arrival. It hurt to sell, but only because I was losing an opportunity for growth. St-Michel wouldn't remain a point of arrival forever. It was still under-valued, but it was getting more attention now that prices in neighboring Villeray were increasing. I was no longer a St-Michel boy. I had outlived that memory, that nostalgia. I was a millionaire with an expanding property management business. I had leveraged my two rental buildings to purchase a 20-room apartment complex in the southeast, down by the river. I planned to own 50 rental units across the island by my 40th birthday. I also started searching for a new home for myself. I was tired of the stuffy Montréal apartments with their old wood, stained glass, creaking floors, their views of fire escapes, clotheslines, and flat rooftops, and the way they allowed the past to leak into every crevice of life.

I wanted a new construction high in the Golden Square Mile district. I wanted to soar. I wanted a 15-foot wall of windows, a massive glass-enclosed terrace overlooking the city, four bedrooms, three marble bathrooms, two floors, a chef's kitchen with an eight-burner gas range, a walk-in closet large enough for a day bed. I wanted storage for a collection of vintages, white leather sectionals, and Persian rugs in every room.

My final afternoon in the house I'd inherited from my grandfather, its rooms empty, I received a notification on my phone. It was a new listing. I'd been browsing listings every night, and so many of the million-dollar homes reflected a kind of generic luxury. I stopped being able to tell them apart, and this one was no different. I swiped through the photos of white rooms until, in the corner of a gleaming salon, I saw a figure. The figure was about three feet tall, black, wearing an antique dinner jacket with polished brass buttons, each one bearing a crescent moon and star. He was holding a large planter in his arms, which were bent at 90 degrees. The planter did indeed hold a plant, a palm whose fronds tumbled down over the head of its carrier. The figure was wearing a fez.

I zoomed in. There he was, in glazed and brilliantly painted porcelain, with the sunlight pouring down through the high windows all around him. His back was straight, his face impassive. I searched the photo for his twin, and then swiped back through the other photos of the listing, but between the Barcelona chairs, glass coffee tables, mahogany armoires, I didn't encounter another figure. I immediately emailed the agent, and I knew that the first question I would ask the seller on my visit would appall my grandfather, "Where did you buy your Nubian?"

If the answer was the correct one, if it mentioned the Ritz, I would follow with the inevitable, "Is he your only one?"

If the seller squirmed or deflected, I would insist, "Can we include them in the price?"

Shooting the General

I'VE ALWAYS ENJOYED detective stories, less so those about American gumshoes who swig bourbon and whose five o'clock shadow entices the femme fatale. I narrowly prefer the European variety, in which the bourbon is replaced by rare vintages, or—in a rakish, synthetic twist— pharmaceuticals, and instead of the protagonist being a self-employed private dick, they're a state-employed dick with elite training in the martial arts, or advanced degrees in mathematics. This is a problem. Another problem with the European variety is the agents, who are often caricatures of the idea of an agent. Their phallic pens double as recording devices or laser beams, their nanotechnological cerebral implants allow them to decode all languages. Their Aston Martins perform best at high speeds, they demonstrate extraordinary skill at the tables of Monaco, they have inexhaustible wardrobes, esoteric knowledge of art and rare gems, and ease with the opposite, and rarely the same, · sex.

For me, the perfect spy must not be a fictional charac- ter. It's someone who must have firsthand experience of the small travails of the daily existence of a people, who must know "the struggle," and must be both defeated by the cause and devoted to it, as I was in 1967, when I was stationed in the Hôtel d'Angleterre, in Lausanne, as part of *Opération Prochain Épisode*.

Lausanne is a difficult set of memories to reassemble, and it is equally difficult to recall the Montréal to which I returned. I do recall returning in disgrace, having failed to shoot the revolutionary H. Aquin, who was attempting to steal a painting titled *The Death of General Wolfe*, depicting a historic colonial battle, and to sell it to an underground dealer for the money to purchase arms. The arms would embolden the struggle for Québec independence. At least, that is the story I was told.

In the painting, which now hangs in the National Gallery in Ottawa, a man lies dying on a plain. He is surrounded by other men, whose expressions range from pensiveness to concern, then from anguish to dejection. In the distance, a column of smoke thickens as it rises. Ships sit in a harbor. Calm, gray-haired military doctors attend to the dying man, while a blurred figure emerges from the background. His hand is raised and his eyes and mouth open toward the person staring into the painting. He wants to say something, he has something to say, he is running toward us. We think we know what he wants to say, we feel its urgency rising in his throat, and we think that if he runs fast enough, if he reaches the side of the dying colonial general, if he blurts his message into the general's white ear, it will restore life, and all of the expressions on the faces of the men around the general will shift, gradually, as his life is restored, from dejection to relief, from anguish to elation, from concern to satisfaction, and from pensiveness to insouciance. The bloodstains will fade from his bandages and the column of smoke will go from gray to white, and drift off like an indifferent cloud. The messenger never arrives, and we confront our instinctive reaction to the suffering of another human being, to the anguish of those close to him. We see the political motivation behind the scene of common suffering: the flag of empire, the red coats, the romance of a death in the service of a cause whose nobility history questions. Why should we want this man to live?

These questions abide, as others arise. What happened to the people in the painting? What happened to the few firsthand witnesses to the death of General Wolfe? Did they disappear into the population? Do their descendants sit in classrooms and on city buses next to the descendants of those who lost the battle? What happened to those men? Did they follow imperial decree and travel across the globe to campaign against the independence of other peoples? Did they disappear into the jungles of South America seeking El Dorado? Do their cobwebbed skeletons decorate the sets of Indiana Jones movies, the frames of Tintin adventure comics? Did they marry into the local culture, and did their great-great-great grandchildren eventually join the *Front de libération du Québec* and plant a bomb in *La Bourse*? I answer that those musket wounds are General Wolfe's wages, and should be paid to him in full. What this image tells me is that the only way to acquire independence is to fight for it. If you are afraid to shoot the general, you are afraid to be free.

When I returned from Lausanne I was not free. I had failed to repatriate the painting. I had failed to kick my addiction to amphetamines and opiates. I returned to a Montréal in which bombs were being planted in mailboxes, foreign diplomats stuffed into car trunks, and the punch cards that fed the Concordia computer center's mainframe floated down from the sky like a rain of mechanical disinformation, while the Caribbean students who accused professor Perry Anderson and their administration of racism barricaded themselves inside and were smoked out with real fire. The television cameras rolled on de Maisonneuve Boulevard and everyone stared up toward the smoking windows. I stood and stared, and I and everyone else knew that we were watching history unfold far above our heads, while some fools in the crowd chanted, "let the niggers burn."

That day I wandered toward Peel Street, and for the first time went down into the newly dug metro tunnels. As I descended, I thought of the word "underground," meaning below the surface of the earth. "Underground" also belongs to the category of adjectives, words that describe or modify a noun, as in: the underground resistance, a site of suppressed or concealed activities, a network of secret operations. But before this turns into another convenient conspiracy theory, I am not part of any network, I do not resist anything. I am underground because in 1968 Thelonious Monk released a jazz album called *Underground*, as the Montréal metro was being built.

On the cover of that album, Monk is sitting at an upright piano, his head turned to his right, looking at the person gazing at him, as if startled by our sudden arrival.

We become conscious of our presence. His hands are spread across the keyboard, and a cigarette rests between his lips. The room looks like a cross between a barn and a cellar, with straw and hay littered across the floorboards, bottles of wine standing on various surfaces, a store of grenades on a table. Monk, surprised mid-song, smoking, has a dynamite detonator at his feet. More important than all of this is the graffiti that says *Vive la France* painted in white on the wall above the head of a Nazi SS officer who is bound with thick rope in the corner. He is still wearing his cap and evil spectacles. Farther back is a woman holding a machine gun, vigilant, her gaze doubling Monk's while passing above his head to meet that of the person who just entered. It seems they are torturing the Nazi with jazz, or realigning his neural pathways using jazz music as the realigning agent. The image so appeals to me because Monk described it as a representation of being in a sort of cultural underground, producing ideas that challenged established norms while living in double obscurity, the darkness of his skin, and the distance from the spotlights, sequins, silver screens, and flashbulbs of popular culture. Monk's cover also carries a message directly opposed to conquest. It does not cast the dying colonial general as a beloved and tragic war hero. The officer is captive while the musician, armed, spreads his fingers across the keyboard.

I thought about all of this as I descended. When I reached the underground I knew that I had arrived. I have never before felt the same thing. Never. Not when a flight I was on landed after its nocturnal passage over the Atlantic. Not even when securely returned to my home country after a decade in Europe and North America. Not when setting foot on the ramp of the Aéroport International Léopold Sédar Senghor, feeling the heat glaze my skin, then looking up and seeing the sky soaring overhead and reflecting: that is the sky over Africa. Not even when I was back inside my boyhood home having dinner with my parents, speaking Wolof peppered with words in Arabic, languages I have always retained while living abroad. I can think of a thousand examples of what most people would identify as "arrival," and the only time I've experienced a sense of this, beyond the common sense of reaching a destination, was when I saw that FOR RENT/À LOUER sign underground, in the Peel metro tunnel.

A combination of things attracted me to the underground, its natural heat and insulation against the winter, of course, and the feeling of being cocooned and protected, whereas outside among the buildings and automobiles a person is exposed. Standing on the street corner waiting for the light to change, a person feels the sharp edge of the wind, and a car slows as it rounds the corner and someone sticks their face out the rear window and spits, *Nègre*.

But here, under all of the concrete, glass, and steel, I have a feeling of being held, and of having time held back. I don't have any idea of the prevailing social attitudes—that isn't entirely true. Reception is poor underground, but I still listen to the radio. I can still get a couple of channels on my Zenith. It's clear to me that times and attitudes change, but I don't have a daily experience of that, and in some ways I don't really care. Time, like fresh air, grows stale about one story below street level.

What replaces time and the urgencies and anxieties it produces in the downtown crowd, in the business day and the fleet week, is the buzz of electricity under the city, a single note drone that never ceases, that can easily fade into the background or that can be concentrated upon. I call it the denominator. It is the sonic denominator of the city, and every time I feel myself turning my head upward and anticipate seeing a flurry of computer punch cards in the air, I recall that note.

I have been in business since I first saw the FOR RENT/À LOUER sign in that storefront in the underground strip mall. I am the sole proprietor of a boutique that sells African art and artifacts. I return to Senegal, my home country—my *former* home country—twice a year to purchase trinkets from street vendors for next to nothing, and I will eventually sell them for exorbitant prices to young people seeking their identity and older people looking to sustain that identity by displaying wooden masks and statues about their homes, or others wishing to proclaim their heritage by wearing beaded bracelets, wrought copper earrings, or by draping patterned cloths over the backs of couches.

The articles undergo a strange transformation in the passage from Senegal to Montréal. They lose something, something inside them stops glowing. Does this sound romantic, sentimental? Objects aren't animate, they don't have feelings in this culture, so can we say that something dies? When the object arrives the context is off, and its meaning is uncertain. It may still have monetary value, and its monetary value may increase, but what does that mean? A black wood mask might be worth 200 dollars in my store. At least, I know that if I price it at 200 dollars I will eventually find someone who will pay that much for it. While it may hang on a living room wall and provide decoration and aesthetic inspiration, beyond that, what does it mean in this city, in this hemisphere?

I can't explain it. The wood grows dim and it acquires a grayish tint. It no longer inhabits an animist cosmology. It has a value, but no essence or soul beyond that value. It is object alone, and on the occasions when I've held an article in my hand during the flight overseas, something inside the wood, some presence, has gradually dimmed, until the object feels heavy and dead in my hands, and this is the case for all of the objects I bring across, all of the objects that make the passage. I would like to be able to reanimate them, but that would require knowledge and abilities beyond what I possess.

It was 1967. I was stationed near the top of the world, high in the cool air at the foot of the Alps. After a morning dose of amphetamines, an espresso and a Gauloise, Lac Léman seemed to burn blue. In its depths I imagined the island of Cuba sinking, its palm trees bending in the electric water, the entire revolutionary land mass settling to the bottom of the lake, and with it the dreams of solidarity among nascent revolutions and emerging nations in Africa, the Caribbean, South America, and even North America. I kept taking pills, amphetamines to speed me up, then stelazine to bring me down. I burned cold and hot. I knew that the person I'd been sent to intercept was doing the same thing in another room in the same hotel, hallucinating the same future sinking in the same body of water. Every room in the Hôtel d'Angleterre contained just such a person trying to balance their nerves before setting out on their assignment. We might be doubled, or trebled, or multiplied to infinity, the possibilities and uncertainties contained within our cortexes increased beyond number, but one thing remained certain: at the appropriate moment we would all emerge from our rooms with our bloodshot eyes concealed behind mirror sunglasses, our frigid narcotic sweat absorbed by our dry-cleaned suits, and our dedication to our particular revolutions intact.

Now I can't remember if Lac Léman wasn't Lake Louise, or Lac aux Castors, some body of water in Banff, or a blue expanse in some other mountain town whose hub is an immense hotel built in the colonial period, built specifically to accommodate royal visits. In hindsight one place becomes another, and any place can become the top of the world, depending on the concentration of the amphetamines.

I was on assignment from the government of a budding nation, one whose independence was perhaps just pretense, or a dream in the minds of men who owned vineyards in France. How could I know that that budding would ripen into a bomb ticking inside a mailbox, a university computer center set afire, and a visiting British diplomat bound and crammed into a trunk?

I used to live above ground like everyone else. I used to walk the streets wearing beautifully tailored suits. I pre-

ferred lighter colors, creams, pale browns, and whites
because they best highlighted my skin. When you are a tall,
dark-skinned Senegalese man in the streets of Montréal,
you have nowhere to hide. It does get tiresome always being conspicuous, always getting noticed, yet always being
treated as if you didn't notice you were being noticed.
People talk about you, point at you, stare openly in spite of
all social taboos. It's strange then, that I would be stationed
as a double agent in Lausanne, the whitest place on earth,
in 1967, but the logic was impeccable. I was so conspicuous
that nobody would imagine I was there to perform a covert
operation. Plus, who in 1967 would believe that an African
could possibly be a double agent?

When I arrived in Lausanne I understood that I wasn't
the only African there. The Hôtel d'Angleterre was full of
other African double agents. We watched each other over
espressos in the restaurant. We glanced over the tops of
upside-down newspapers and adjusted our Moscot spectacles. We stood slowly and smoothed our suits, then
glanced about the room to see who was watching, tucked
our Italian newspapers under our arms, and headed into
the bright day.

Yes, this business of being underground is indeed
consistent with my former life of espionage. I grew accustomed to never being who I appeared to be, allowing
people to think one thing while using their perception as
a veil. Every immigrant knows this. People might think
that you are poor, that you come from some little country
sweltering by the equator, and that you have nature
but not culture, naked beauty instead of wealth. They

don't need to know that you and your brother own the apartment building where they rent, or that your children are studying to become doctors while theirs are studying art history. They don't need to know. Who are they?

I live underground to get away from them. Every day at 9 am I open up my African boutique in the corridor that leads to Peel metro station. I light my incense, put on my Persol aviator sunglasses, the ones with mirror lenses, and let the intricate and infinite syncopations of Fela Kuti's Africa '70 entice—or repel—the passersby. I sit behind the glass showcase-counter, surrounded by images of ancient gods and mythic figures that this society knows nothing about, and I prepare to do business. Nobody knows me. Nobody recognizes me. Nobody walks into my store and, as they are about to ask the price of a wooden giraffe, breathlessly exclaims: "You're... you're... Hamidou Diop!"

Dominoes at the Crossroads

Dans une île tropicale, de jeunes révolutionnaires décident de tuer l'homme chargé de réprimer les soulèvements populaires. Leur premier acte de liberté ...

I WAS IN THE Librairie Gallimard on St-Laurent Boulevard, scanning the jacket summary of Édouard Glissant's *La Lézarde* when Tamika called. She had just seen a CBC travel warning about the island we were preparing to visit. Several tenant farmers armed with machetes, spades, and shovels attempted to storm the property of a landowner. I slid *La Lézarde* back onto the shelf and went outside to talk. One man had been shot, while dogs had mauled another. The report was for a different part of the island than the one we would be visiting, and CBC stressed that the military had been deployed. I nonetheless reassured Tamika that I had roots there, I understood the culture, and I would be able to read the people.

We would be staying with my cousin Erroll, who was 15 years older than me. He was born on the island but as a teen he'd moved to England, where he'd started an independent record label to promote the island's music. As the music gained in popularity he traveled the world producing albums and promoting concerts. He later ran the business with his wife Irene, a Londoner whose parents were attorneys. Irene lived to visit the ashrams of India, sleep under the Sahara's stars, kayak deep into the rainforests of Thailand. The couple eventually sold the label to Chris Blackwell in a deal that was reported in *Rolling Stone*. They bought land on a hill in the island's countryside, built a two-story home, and relocated. In keeping with the local fashion, the home was concrete, painted white and cream with terra cotta shingles, Roman columns, and a wide veranda overlooking green hills.

Erroll picked us up from the airport. His dreadlocks hung loose as he chatted about the home studio he was building. We drove through the center of town during the midday rush. Tourists strolled the boulevards. Traffic backed up all the way through town. Soldiers stood observing intersections with rifles held against their chests. Teenage girls dressed in short-shorts, flip-flops, and torn tank tops sold bananas car to car. Erroll bought two bunches, then said it was best to avoid shopping in town, where the prices were inflated. Music from the island-themed bars competed with car horns, vendors' voices, and motorbike engines. Dust and unfiltered exhaust mixed with the heat. Inside the bars, tourists sat at lottery machines and drank mojitos. Gradually the traffic thinned and the road narrowed to one lane. Erroll wove around potholes, stopped for goats, and slowed to greet street vendors with a shout. Trees and tangled bush rose up. The road inclined, then swung back down as we entered the hills. Green rushed past our windows and the damp air rolled through the car. Erroll pulled up to a crossroads that housed a cluster of rustic shops and a restaurant.

We wandered in and out of a few places, picking up bottled water and a meal that consisted of curry goat, rice and peas, and shaved cabbage. We also bought star apples, oranges, and june plums from a street vendor. We pretended at relaxation, but the locals watched us closely, with their stern, sun-hammered faces, and barely acknowledged us when we smiled or said hello. A group of men sitting at a low table playing dominoes paused their game and followed us with their eyes. I said hello, knowing that my accent would be familiar. One of them grunted and curled his lip, revealing the glint of a gold tooth.

In a corner store, where all of the goods were held behind an iron grille, and the money and purchases were exchanged through a small hatch that the clerk opened and closed accordingly, two men leaned up against a side wall. One watched my hand as it slid into my pocket to extract a bill. The other made a subtle kissing gesture toward Tamika and whispered, "brownin," and when I looked at him he looked away, but allowed a sly smile to twist the corner of his mouth. In the low-ceilinged restaurant, which sweated the smell of stewing meat, and which was really a shack, we waited on our order as men with bleary eyes wandered into a bar at the back. It was dark, and only the glow from the video lottery machines lit the room. We were served by an elderly lady with a smooth black face whose voice was soft with us, but which rose and sharpened the instant she turned back to the kitchen.

Erroll drove the switchback road up to the house with

one hand on the wheel of his BMW, hugging the curves, talking over the music, and leaving only inches between his car and several schoolgirls walking in a line. We listened, and when we finally slowed before the gate, six lean German Shepherds lunged toward us barking. Erroll barked back. The dogs retreated, the gate slid open, and we drove up to the cream house. The dogs lay down under the fruit trees, eyeing the road. We sat on the veranda and stared at the hills.

It had rained earlier that morning. A mist veiled the hills, and dense cloud swelled behind them. We spent hours watching the inert, sweeping curves dressed in green, our eyes following their contours, our eyes absorbing their vibrant color. Some of the hills seemed untouched, not a single house on them, no strip cut from the forest, just plants overgrowing themselves. I thought that it was therapeutic to look at the green, to concentrate on the point where the foliage flared into the steelpan blue of the sky. High above, the odd hawk or eagle circled, riding a current of air.

Tamika, from behind her wide sunglasses, noted, "Those villagers didn't seem too friendly."

"No. They didn't. That's one thing that always makes it difficult to visit this place, that you always stand out. It's unnerving."

"It is, but you're simplifying things. You look like you might have roots here, but it's your light skin, your linen shirts, and khaki pants from the Bay, it's your braided leather loafers, which I love, and it's your 400 dollar Cutler and Gross sunglasses. It's in your walk and the way you carry yourself—"

"Yeah, and it's obvious the second *you* open your mouth." I sounded more aggressive than I intended, but Tamika ignored it.

"Sure. It's both of us. It's in our posture and the shape of our mouths, the way we walk up before we even say a word. I think part of the perceived hostility is people just trying to figure out what our background is, they're just curious."

"Hmm."

"So you can relax a bit, and that will also put people at ease."

"I don't like it." For some reason I felt entitled to my frustration.

"Justifiably so. This is country, man. Some people here don't have electricity. No work. They play dominoes the whole day. They've spent their lives here, and you're a wealthy high brown international with nice clothes and a pocket full of bills, relaxing up in the hills."

"And a brownin' with me. You think I don't know my own country?"

Tamika opened a book. "You said it."

"I wonder if the Wi-Fi works or if we'll have to use our data—"

The dogs leaped up and bolted to the gates barking. Outside the gates, an elderly shepherd with a white T-shirt on his head, under a battered baseball cap, accompanied a herd of goats past the house. The dogs barked for a while, then settled back down in the shade. The dust of their own agitation settled over them. The goats paused to graze, then continued with the herd, then stopped to graze again. The shepherd was patient, as if this pace of grazing and wandering was ingrained. At one point he looked up to the house, and we waved from the veranda. He seemed to hesitate for a moment and consider something, then he gave us a curt wave and returned to his herd. The shepherd seemed not to notice the heat. He worked slowly and easily, sometimes stopping to lean on his tall walking stick, exposed to the sun, while we sweated in the shade of the white veranda.

"I'm going for a swim."

"Mmm." Tamika didn't look up from her book. She was researching the Grenada revolution, and once we returned to the city, she would be working from the main university campus. Part of her research involved talking with scholars and journalists who wrote about the revolution as it was unfolding. She was also interviewing people who attempted to resettle in Grenada. A week before we left, she watched a documentary on Netflix called *The House on Coco Road*, about an African American woman who moved her young family to Grenada during the revolution. After the American invasion in 1983, and the murder of Maurice Bishop, the family was airlifted out. Tamika was reading everything she could about Maurice Bishop, his predecessor Eric Gairy, the New Jewel Movement, the revolution, and the subsequent invasion. She was moved by the many foreigners—Canadians, Brits, Americans, and Caribbeans—who relocated to Grenada in the early 1980s, their politics invigorated by the promise of a society based explicitly on the principles of Black liberation. By 1980, Tamika's parents, both of whom were journalists, had left

Grenada and landed in Scarborough, and because of the 1983 invasion, they didn't visit Grenada again until 2015.

The dogs followed me to the pool, and when they didn't receive any food, they slumped down under the breadfruit trees, and I stared over the azure water, then dove in. I felt the cool water rush over me, felt my lungs strain as I swam laps. After several laps I paused and floated. A gray-blue heron skulked among the poolside bush. It froze, leapt up onto one leg, balanced for a second, then darted its neck down into the bush. When it straightened back up it held a small iguana in its beak. The iguana wriggled as the heron crunched and swallowed it. The heron continued padding through the low bush.

After several more laps I strolled up to the veranda. Tamika was looking toward the gate. Erroll was talking to four men who had disembarked from an old, roofless brown jeep. One man stood in front while the other three stood back and listened. They stared up to the house, at us sitting on the veranda, and at Irene, framed by the front door. The man gestured assertively, his voice raised, but Erroll seemed calm. He shook his head, raised his hands, then stepped forward and pointed. They talked for about five minutes, and finally Erroll bumped fists with the man, who jumped into the back seat. The other three men slowly embarked, letting their eyes linger on the house, on Irene, and on us. The jeep chugged and sputtered, and left a cloud of blue smoke behind.

"Who were those guys?" Tamika took off her sunglasses and squinted.

Erroll pushed his locks back from his face. "Yeah, they

do some work for me on the property. You might see them some mornings this week." He paused, and added, "If you see them pull up, come get me, nuh?" We nodded. Farther down the hill the jeep slowed and idled next to the shepherd. He leaned on his walking stick, which was cut from a single crooked branch, about seven feet tall, the top of it standing above him as if signaling to someone in the distance. The four men in the jeep leaned toward him and gestured, but he seemed cool against his stick. He looked back up at the house, at us sitting on the veranda, and then he turned toward his goats.

"Those guys didn't seem too happy. You were in the pool, but I think Erroll gave them money."

"He did say they work for him."

"Do you believe that?"

"Why shouldn't I?"

"I suppose it's possible."

"It is. They probably do all kinds of landscaping, painting, and other jobs for him. Look at the size of this place."

"Still, they didn't seem happy."

"What happened?"

"They drove up, and the dogs ran down and started barking, and then the driver looked up at me and smiled, then pointed two fingers at the dogs, in a gunshot gesture, and pretended to shoot them, one by one."

"What?"

"For real."

"It was a joke?"

"How would I know?"

I wanted to reassure us both that it was a rough joke, but I couldn't. I squinted across at the hills. Tamika continued, "Once he was done, he shouted for Erroll, several times, and just as I was about to knock on the door, Erroll popped out. He looked a bit annoyed, but he was like, 'it's cool, cool.' He had a brown envelope in his hand, which he passed through the bars. The man looked into the envelope and then they started arguing. The other guys jumped out of the jeep and stood up behind their friend, then you came up from the pool and you saw the rest."

The dogs were slumped in the shade again, but their heads were up, ears cocked. They watched the front gate. In light of everything Tamika was recounting, I was secretly thankful for their presence. I reasoned, "All I saw was a discussion, and whatever you saw could easily have been a disagreement between an employer and employees. Maybe they asked him for a raise, or they were discussing a schedule. Erroll can handle it."

"How do you know that?"

I didn't know, but I kissed my teeth in mock-annoyance and looked at the books on the table. One of them was *Triangular Road*, by Paule Marshall. Tamika caught me eyeing the book. "There's an interesting passage about Grenada in th—"

"I don't need the revolution now," I interrupted.

Tamika disappeared behind her sunglasses, their lenses reflecting green hills. Down the dirt road, the shepherd and his goats were gone.

I woke up sweating. My forehead had soaked my pillow. My shirt was wet. I drank some water and went to the window. The dogs were silent, the front gate was locked, the hills were still, and the leaves shivered in the breeze. I went out to the veranda to listen to the hiss of the crickets.

I'd been reading *La Lézarde*, in which a group of young militants plot the murder of a repressive politician, a story that immediately recalled the 1970 October Crisis in Montréal. I'd fallen asleep wondering about similarities in the conversations between Montréal's French militants and the ones Glissant imagined between Martinique's fictional militants. The reimagined conversations were punctuated by the dogs barking in the yard. I couldn't figure out why they were barking. It could be a shepherd passing with his herd. It could be someone on the road, walking. It could be a car climbing the hillside. It could be anything. But why would a shepherd be out in the middle of the night? Who would be walking at this hour? Who else lived out past the house?

I woke up sweating again. The dogs were excitable. I reassured myself that Erroll and Irene would hear them, and would surely look into things. But Erroll and Irene were so accustomed to hearing them that they no longer listened. I stood up in the dark room. What was the purpose of having guard dogs who barked at everything? I was naked, so I pulled on a pair of jeans and a belt. Sleep still hung over me as I walked to the window and parted the drapes. The dogs were barking at the gate. Some were jumping up and others were running back and forth, but I couldn't see beyond the gate. I couldn't see who was there.

As I undid the bolt on the door it clanked and woke Tamika. "It's ok Tamma I'm just getting some air. Bad dream. It's ok." She sat up rubbing her eyes, and I wondered whether she'd had a nightmare as well.

The dogs were still firing volleys of noise from their throats, and I thought I heard low voices coming from somewhere just out of sight beyond the gates. I squatted down on the veranda and looked out from between the railing posts. I waited, and I heard it: the low grumble of an engine, the sound of gravel crunching under tires. Then I heard voices, just above a whisper. I couldn't make out any words, but I knew that I had to go back into the room and tell Tamika, then wake Erroll and Irene. I didn't know whether I knew this or my dream knew it, and I squatted there deliberating the provenance of this knowledge. This was an important distinction to make, because it would determine whether the rebels were really there. I looked down and realized that I was naked again.

I was back in bed, opening my eyes to the blue room and hearing a fusillade of barking outside. I lay there and listened to the dogs, and it pissed me off that they were so hysterical and undisciplined. Every time there was slight movement outside the gates, the dogs leaped, lunged, barked, growled at the bars. They even did this at night, so we had all learned to ignore them. How could we distinguish between a genuine alarm and a false one? Did someone need to rush outside each time the dogs made noise in the night? Should I go outside? I was naked, and warm, but I knew that I should at least go to the window and look.

Instead of getting up, I turned my eyes to the door. It was a hollow panel of plywood, with a deadbolt and an additional bolt lock on the inside. It was the only thing that would stand between us and the rebels, once they breached the gate. Erroll had confirmed the alarmist news reports: rebels were seizing all of the land in the area. Much of it had recently been bought by wealthy internationals, but all of this land had once lain idle. It belonged to the local government. Farmers grazed their animals, people squatted the land and picked fruit, until successful islanders from England and America, seduced by the idea of an inexpensive island home away from the condos and time-shares of the tourist towns, started buying up and fencing in the land, building houses that they didn't occupy— houses whose construction they didn't always complete. Unpainted concrete shells stood, scoured by the sun and rain, slowly infiltrated by green.

A group of men who spent their days playing dominoes at the crossroads, some of whom had deserted the military when it couldn't pay their wages, and who were now idle, decided to put their old fatigues back on, drive from property to property, and demand a "security tax" from the owners on the hill.

The men—the rebels—drove a rusted army jeep whose suspension creaked. It gave them an air of rugged militancy. At first the new landowners were compliant. The sum the rebels demanded was so small they paid it without objection, almost with an appreciation for the comedic dishevelment of the operation. The rebels were insulted by how easily the landowners paid. They became embarrassed by their failure to provoke even a raised eyebrow. They demanded more, brusquely insisted, brandished their dulled cutlasses. Loud arguments with landowners ensued, and there were fights at the crossroads when they swaggered into the bar with their pockets full.

A frustrated landowner, an attorney born on the island who now lived and worked in Miami, shot and killed one of the unarmed rebels. The attorney fled back to the States, and news spread to the capital. It captured front page headlines. Several men from neighboring towns appeared at the crossroads, some of whom had worked the offshore oil rigs near Trinidad and Guyana, and who had returned and blown their earnings on a spree. Others were tenant farmers exasperated with their constant arrears. Yet others were unemployed men from the neighboring towns. Some of them walked to the crossroads, some rode motorcycles, and a small group drove in another old military jeep. They held their meetings over white rum in the rear of the restaurant, in the glow of the lottery machines.

Early one evening the two jeeps crept up the hill to the American attorney's property. It was seized, his dogs were shot, and his housekeeper and groundskeeper, both islanders earning a subsistence wage, were given a few cautionary blows and turned loose. From then on, the rebels used his property as their encampment, from which they could control access to and from the crossroads. The rebels sent out a jeep full of armed men to inform all of the neighboring landowners that the road belonged to them, and a toll had to be paid for passage. They set up a checkpoint so that anyone entering or exiting could be subjected to their whims, which added insult, search, and seizure of goods to the payment of tolls.

The seizure happened the same evening that we landed on the island. We were sitting reading at Erroll's when it happened, and from that moment we became prisoners in Erroll's white house. Each day the rebels drove up to Erroll's property to demand money, water, food, or other amenities, and we knew it was just a matter of time before the local military intervened, or the rebels scattered, or they decided to seize another property farther up the hill, closer to ours. We slept in shifts and waited.

I felt heat on my face and a brightness just beyond my eyelids. I was slumped to the side in a plastic deck chair, still on the veranda. The sun was rising, stretching pink beams across the hills. *La Lézarde* was open in my lap. A mist hung over the hills and evaporated as it rose. I drifted back to sleep for a few seconds, thinking about how the fronds deflected the sun's fire, and how cool and moist it must be beneath them. My head lolled, and I jerked up. I looked down at the papers on the mosaic table and read:

MANIFESTO OF THE
NEW JEWEL MOVEMENT
FOR POWER TO THE PEOPLE
AND FOR ACHIEVING REAL
INDEPENDENCE FOR GRENADA,
CARRIACOU, PETIT MARTINIQUE
AND THE GRENADIAN GRENADINES (1973)

ALL THIS HAS GOT TO STOP

Introduction

The people are being cheated and have been cheated for too long—cheated by both parties, for over twenty years. Nobody is asking what the people want. We suffer low wages and higher cost of living while the politicians get richer, live in bigger houses and drive around in even bigger cars. The government has done nothing to help people build decent houses; most people still have to walk miles to get water to drink after 22 years of politicians....

It continued. Its angular language jarred me awake. I tiptoed into the room where Tamika was sprawled across the bed. I sat up next to her and wondered what the hell we were doing back on the Island. I knew that in the eyes of the locals, the men and women down by the crossroads, the shepherd on the hill, and the men in the beat-up jeep, I was soft and wealthy. When I looked over at my cheap 40-dollar linen shirts from the Bay, I felt so carefully groomed, so contrived that I ached to return to the capital, to the campus where Tamika would be doing her research on the New Jewel Movement and the revolution. Our academic interest in a revolution in the Caribbean now seemed like an entitled desire, and we were like children romanticizing toy soldiers. We knew nothing of the guerilla's existence, knew nothing of the vertiginous green of the steaming jungle. We were here playing, and that became clear the moment the plane settled on the taxiway and a chorus of women exclaimed praises to the Lord, broke into applause, and we began to feel a connection to our roots. Even that "connection" seemed suspect, one born of privilege, something we could purchase with a trip to the island, gripe about, and then renew with another purchase.

The dogs were barking again. I cursed and swung my legs off the bed. Tamika muttered: "What's the matter?"

"Nothing, don't worry." I went to the window. The dogs were dashing back and forth, and some were leaping up in front of the gate. It was still early and the heat hadn't yet risen, so I pulled on a pair of jeans, a linen shirt, and went back out to the veranda. The dogs seemed to be moving through liquid air, jumping in slow arcs, baring their teeth and snapping at the bars, and I was momentarily mesmerized by them. I stood watching, still with sleep in my mind, when I heard the rusted chug of an old engine. I waited as the dogs barked, and then the brown jeep appeared, and the dogs went wild, snapping between the bars, dashing up to the front steps and barking at the door, then dashing back. Four men were in the jeep, along with an arsenal of spades, hoes, and pick-axes. The driver leveled two fingers at the dogs and took aim. He pretended to fire a slow shot, then a second, a third, a fourth. After each shot, he paused, blew air over his fingers, and took aim at another dog.

I froze on the veranda. *La Lézarde* was splayed open, face up. The cover image was taken from a watercolor. In the background was an indistinct mass of vegetation painted a metallic blue. A branching power line stood in front, with cables running to the edges of the cover. A humble pink box-house stood next to the power line, with a crooked window, and in the foreground a male figure in shorts and straw sun-hat, slightly bent, trudging by. His shadow stretched behind him. The scene looked relaxed, idyllic, and yet despondent. That man could have been one of the rebels who gathered at the crossroads, one of the armed men sleeping in the sun at the checkpoint.

I locked the door behind me. Erroll was on the step, already sliding into his flip-flops, with his dreadlocks dangling around his head and tumbling over his shoulders. He looked tired.

"Yeah, yeah, ah come just now, just now," he said to nobody in particular. He barked at the dogs, and their acrobatics immediately ceased. They retreated into the shade and lay down, but they kept their heads up, ears pricked. He waved to the men in the grumbling jeep, and pressed the remote to open the gate. It groaned and swung open. The driver waved and turned the jeep up the drive. The men hopped out as Erroll greeted them. They shouted and waved to me, and I waved back. The men unloaded their tools and followed Erroll into the yard.

Witness

I WAS SMOKING on the veranda when Quammie returned from his day trip to Berbice. Everyone pronounced it *Borbeace*, bending the vowels while digging deep into the first syllable. He had gone out with Uncle Koffi, Auntie Shanice, and Calvin, the driver. They went to visit our cousin Calib, who had spent decades in a state-run asylum. They packed clothes and chocolate for him, and since the other patients might try to steal both the clothes and the chocolate, they brought enough chocolate to share with everyone.

When Auntie Shanice asked if I wanted to go, I declined. I spent the day in downtown Georgetown. I wandered. I got my hair faded at an open-air barbershop. I absorbed the heat and the compressed cacophony of the city. I spent an hour and the equivalent of a hundred U.S. dollars at a bookstore that had a large collection of Caribbean writers, the kind of collection that can't be found in Canada. I returned just after dusk, and sat outside leafing through Mittelholzer, Nichols, and Walcott. The humidity softened my cigarette, and the smoke thickened in my throat.

It was too early to drink, so I read and waited for the others to return. I stayed back because I didn't know Calib.

I didn't want him to feel embarrassed by his circumstances, but I was curious. When the electric gates creaked open and the car rolled into the drive, I stood and motioned for Quammie to join me on the veranda. He came up, sat back on one of the mahogany deck chairs, closed his eyes, and let out a long sigh. I balanced my cigarette on the ashtray.

"How was the visit?"

He kept his eyes closed and his head tilted back. His face was greased from the heat. I waited. Finally, he spoke without opening his eyes. "It was disturbing, actually, I don't want to talk about it."

He stood up and went inside. I heard some bumping around, a door closing, and he re-emerged with a Banks beer. "Mostly it was flat, brown, yellow, green. We spent a lot of time in a hot car."

"I figured."

"Is that why you didn't come?"

"No. I figured it might be overwhelming for him to see so many people. I didn't want to intrude."

"What did you do?"

"Got faded. Explored Georgetown." Quammie motioned for me to turn my head. I did.

"Very nice. Tomorrow you'll show me where. Did you get anything?"

I pointed to the books on the table. "What about you, any tourist souvenirs from Berbice?"

He laughed. "No." Then he pointed to his head and said: "Just up here. I don't know how I'll sleep tonight."

"Was it that bad?"

"I don't want to talk about it yet."

"Ok. Uh, did the rally start before you left, or did you get out of Berbice before it started?"

"The rally," he groaned. He leaned his head back and looked up at the silhouette of a tree. "We got out just fine, no traffic, but on the way back we passed the president's motorcade."

"Whoa. You saw Ramotar?"

"No, I just saw his car."

It was rare that a Guyanese election made international ripples. Uncle Koffi had been feeding me copies of the local paper, the *Stabroek News*, and I'd gleaned that oil had been discovered in the ocean. Guyana and Venezuela were debating whose waters the deposits were submerged in. Exxon had planted a massive offshore rig outfitted with a helipad. Venezuela was threatening to fight over the oil, and was preparing to mobilize troops along the border. Ministers stood to grow rich, and the temperature of the debates rose. Many people feared violence if the election adhered to the country's racial divides. Several shops downtown had already boarded up, and the challenger David Granger's Georgetown headquarters was under armed guard. He'd been nicknamed "Danger" in an attack ad that flashed an image of rolling dice. Jimmy Carter, 90 years old, was expected in Guyana to advocate for a peaceful electoral process. The polls were predicting a narrow loss for Ramotar, who had decreed a state media blackout on all ads and coverage for his rival. That very night, one week out from the election, Ramotar was holding a large rally in Berbice.

"As we were leaving the area, we noticed cars pulled to the shoulder, and people, and bicycles, and goats all standing still, and then a cop stepped into the middle of the road and flagged us, so we pulled over as well. He didn't give us any explanation, so Uncle Koffi leaned out his window and asked another driver what was going on, and they said: 'Ramotar. E comin troo.'"

"We sat in the car for five minutes. Nothing happened. The sun started going down, and across the Savannah you could hear those night sounds start up, but quietly, all of the whistles and chirps, and then the crickets hissing. We got out of the car and waited, and more cars were flagged over to the shoulder, and then a murmur ran through the crowd, and as it approached us people turned and said that Ramotar's motorcade was on its way, it was coming. We squinted as far up the road as we could, stood on our toes, and sure enough there was a black speck vibrating in the distance, and it got closer, louder. The single speck divided into multiple vehicles, motorcycles in the lead, then a series of black vans, then more motorcycles. We were on something of a low hill, so as they approached we could see their entire file. Behind the first group of motorcycles was a long black SUV, with Guyanese flags flying from the front headlights. That must have been Ramotar's car, because behind it were smaller SUVs and sedans."

Quammie slid one of the Matinées out of the pack and lit it. It was dark on the veranda and the night was breathing around us. I saw a thin yellow lizard on the wall above my brother's head, but I didn't say anything. I could see its narrow flanks pulsing to the sounds of crickets and frogs. The odd street dog barked in the distance, and I thought of going to the fridge and grabbing two Guinness, but Quammie interrupted the thought.

"I mean, we could see the motorcade approaching, and it was going fast, like over 120, fast. A goat wandered into the road and stopped, with its head down, licking at something."

"A goat?"

"Yeah. A fucking goat. The same scrawny goat we saw in New Amsterdam, the kind we saw on our way in from the airport. The kind of tough goat we see browsing in a ditch, or tied to a stake in someone's yard. It was yellowish-white, and it just wandered out into the road. An old Indian guy started shouting at the goat, but he didn't go into the road because there was a cop in front of him. He kept shouting at the goat, then speaking to it and pleading with it, then making these soft kissing noises and beckoning in a gentle voice like: 'Come ere, come, come ere, come, come...' and then cooing like a pigeon while gesturing fiercely, but the goat was preoccupied. It kept its head down and licked at the road. I don't know if it was a stupid goat or not, but at one point it noticed the motorcade. It twitched. We could all feel the vibrations through the road, we could feel the speed of the engines. It stood still and looked up, its ears perked, and seconds later two motorcycles roared past it, one on either side, and I swear I saw the goat's body shake with the speed of the bikes. It stood and blinked for a second, and then—as if it hadn't noticed anything—it took a few lazy steps and stopped again, put its head back down, and licked at the road. The Indian guy intensified his cooing, and everyone by the roadside seemed to collectively cringe. The goat looked around just as Ramotar's SUV appeared."

I fell into an old memory of when we were kids. The car radio was playing. Quammie was asleep. My father reached for the volume knob as the car slowed. Chaka Khan's voice faded down into the engine's hum. My mother strained to see above the line of cars stretching ahead of us. We inched along, two slow lanes of traffic, until a Parks Canada ranger in his green and khaki uniform waved the cars over to the right.

"It must be an accident."

"Or construction."

"I don't see any construction signs."

My brother groggily came to, as I looked out my window. The shoulder dropped off into a shallow ravine, and beyond that a curtain of evergreens rose.

The cars rolled in stops and starts. We passed another park ranger who was standing next to a brown pickup with yellow lettering, and then my father said "ooh" under his breath, and my mother inhaled sharply through her teeth. They were looking ahead and to the left. My mother twisted in her seat and told us not to look outside.

I wanted to look, so I ignored the instructions and pressed my face to the window. It was cool and dotted with raindrops. Our Oldsmobile advanced, along with the sedans and station wagons ahead of us.

We approached a mass of contorted metal immobile in the left lane. As we crept past, its form seemed to twist and lengthen until it resembled a blue BMW. Its side-windows were shattered. The front and rear doors on the passenger side were driven inward, into a V shape. The back wheels looked thin and unsteady, as if they might collapse. Two children sat in the back seat, grimacing. Their faces trembled, as if they had tensed up so suddenly in anticipation of impact that their bodies still clung to that tension and would not release it. I was close enough to see their mouths. Their lips were drawn back and their teeth looked like they were about to chatter. The mother was in the passenger seat turned all the way around, restrained by her seatbelt but reaching out to her children. The father was in the drivers' seat, with both hands still on the steering wheel and his head leaning limply forward, a gash along his hairline.

Our windows were up, and the highway scene rolled by like a silent movie. The BMW's windshield was crushed inwards, with a hole larger than a human head in front of the passenger seat. I think my dad slowed down as we passed their car, or maybe the images just appear to me in slow motion now, but I wouldn't put it past my father to slow down and take a long look, wincing while trying to absorb every detail.

The front end of the car was crumpled, and a few meters from the car, which looked like it had been launched backward by the impact, lay a moose. It shivered, and one of its legs twitched. Its legs were spindly, its neck was corded with muscle, and its face was long and sloping, a solid mass of bone covered in coarse fur. Not an ounce of superfluous flesh quivered along its thighs or flanks. As the moose lay there, its massive ribs lifted and fell quickly.

Its glazed eye stared up as the clouds changed shapes and lumbered along.

Quammie continued, "I mean, the van didn't even slow down. It didn't swerve, it didn't brake, nothing. It kept straight on course, and when it hit the goat—"

Neither of us blinked. Our expressions were mirrors of incredulity. Then we guffawed. Our laughter grew louder and rolled down the veranda. We laughed until we were bent over in our chairs, until our sides ached, until tears squeezed out of our eyes and our breath came in a pitched wheeze, and then we settled back and I said: "Fucking Guyana," and we started laughing again.

"When the SUV licked the goat, I swear it seemed like it was happening in slow motion, but the van was going fast. It hit the goat's hind leg, like high on the ass, and the goat flew up in the air and flipped—"

We both nearly fell off our chairs laughing, and again our voices tumbled the length of the veranda and disturbed the night. My brother's eyebrows were raised and he was sitting forward on his chair.

"It fucking flipped up in the air," here he drew a quick flipping motion in the air with his fingers, "and then it fell back down and landed just off the shoulder of the road, but it landed on its feet, and I swear to fucking god it started running while it was still in the air, its legs pumping, because the second its feet hit the ground it bolted into the bush," here he shot his hand forward, holding the cigarette. The ash shook but didn't fall, "and it vanished, like it was swallowed by the bush. The leaves shook behind it and then went still, as if nothing had disturbed them. Then the rest of the motorcade passed. It passed so fast that the little flags on the cars were stiff."

"Whoa."

"Yeah."

The frogs' high nocturnal whistling grew louder and seemed to encircle us. I glanced down the drive and noticed that the streetlights had come on. Mosquitos sizzled around the porch light, and a large moth spread its soft, oil-tinted wings on the white ceiling of the veranda.

"As we drove back, at intervals Calvin would start shaking his head and would bang a fist into the steering wheel and exclaim: 'Man! They ain't even slow the damn car! Straight through! They ain't swerve, nothing! Man!' Koffi and Shanice sighed these painful sighs every time Calvin exclaimed. They hardly said anything all the way back."

The night settled around us, its sleeping trees and leaves breathing slowly to the crickets. Beyond the bushes in the yard was the concrete fence, the spool of razorwire atop it, the electric gate. We heard a muffled, thudding music approaching, and a car crept by, its lights prowling the semi-paved street, its suspension creaking with the unevenness of the road. We watched the car as we smoked, and then Quammie stood up and asked me if I wanted anything. He disappeared inside, and moments later I heard dub music, a record called *Vital Force Dub* by a Nigerian artist. The music was sparse and ominous with heavy low end and sounds delaying and echoing in stereo, but true to its genre it was buoyed by its rhythm. I listened, feeling a curious sensation of being in two places at once.

Quammie stepped back onto the verandah and placed two bottles on the table. He then slid a photo out of his shirt pocket and pressed it down next to the bottles. He pointed and said, "That's him."

It was an old photo. Calib stood in a brown field in front of a long building. The building was low, concrete, institutional, with cracks running up the walls. He was wearing an oversized white T-shirt, and beneath it he looked gaunt. In his narrow face I recognized my own. We must have inherited it from the same distant ancestors, a face in which the African, Chinese, and Portuguese were mixed in equal proportions, and each was visible in a different feature. He had tight red curls, almond-shaped eyes set at an angle, wide lips and flared nostrils, freckles across the bridge of his nose, bronze skin, and a stretched smile that looked like it was unsuited to his face, an expression he rarely made, but recalled from an earlier period in his life. His teeth were long and yellow, and his smile seemed too genuine. I had only seen such unreserved smiles on children, or on elderly people who had languished in care facilities and who, removed from regular social interaction, had forgotten themselves.

I listened to the whistle of the frogs as it rode above the cicadas. Quammie exhaled and stubbed out his cigarette, "When we were leaving, a group of inmates—or patients, whatever—swarmed us and demanded chocolate. At first I didn't know what was going on and I tensed up. Calvin was tense too, but Auntie Shanice was like, 'Be cool, be cool, here, here you go,' and she shared out the extra chocolate while talking to the patients. The asylum staff stood by, watchful." He leaned over, took the photo from the table, remarked, "that's an old picture, he doesn't look like that anymore," and slipped it back into his pocket.

"Once the chocolate was gone Uncle Koffi gave us a discreet nod and pointed toward the parking lot. Calib had hung back during the chocolate rush, but while the staff was preoccupied with dispersing the patients, which really meant barking at them and handling them in a way that was just rough enough to command respect but not rough enough to bruise anyone, Calib slipped away. We found him at the edge of the grounds, out by the parking lot, pacing. He hugged each of us and insisted that we bring out our phones and take more snapshots. Several minutes went by, and noone wanted to break off the engagement, until one of the employees strolled past and noticed Calib. The employee sternly called him over. Calib didn't budge. The employee called for support. Calib backed away just as two more employees appeared, their faces seized with concern. None of us could stand to watch Calib rebuked and manhandled—"

Quammie stood up and turned toward the door, then he stopped. The last thing he said before he went to sleep was that when our cousin was hovering at the edge of the grounds, and no employee had yet noticed his absence, he felt a surge of excitement, and he knew his cousin Calib felt the same thing, a realization that they could rush him into the car and drive off. Quammie looked at Uncle Koffi, at Auntie Shanice, and at Calvin. Their eyes all confirmed the same thought, and they froze.

Petit Marronage

JAZZ JOURNALISTS OFTEN ask me when I first became interested in music, and what attracted me to the saxophone. The question baffles me. I don't remember. I let my silence interrupt the interview, and I cast my thoughts back, but my mind doesn't grasp anything.

If I pick up my alto saxophone, which I rarely play anymore, it feels like a toy in my hands. It's so much smaller than the tenor. My breath fills it easily, and the action of its keys is swift. As I blow, I always picture a lush vine sprouting from the bell of the horn, tumbling to the floor, and slithering across the floor until the ground is covered in leaves. The vine climbs the walls and the ceiling, punches through glass and covers the side of the building, and as the vine grows I can't stop playing. Some greater force controls my fingers and keeps pushing my breath through the horn. I don't think of the notes I'm playing, I just let the process overtake me, until I'm standing in a tropical forest, and I know that lizards hide on the shady underside of leaves, monkeys watch from up in the trees, where the sunlight breaks through and streams down. It's damp and cool, and the plant life seems to breathe with me. Each time I press a key a thousand leaves sprout. Each time I move into a higher register a swarm of insects issues from the horn. They escape into the light and the mist. The vine keeps slithering out of the horn as I blow. I am back to where my ancestors might have marooned, after they were introduced to the Caribbean's plantations.

This is one place my alto saxophone takes me. It has taken me to the floor of the Atlantic Ocean, to a remote cabin that might have inspired a story by Harriet Beecher Stowe, even to a different hemisphere. It may transport me to places that are not in my family history but to which I have some connection, through the sweep of the diaspora.

I don't remember what attracted me to music. My parents tell me I was afraid of the loud drums in the blues and reggae records they spun when I was a child, that I always gravitated to quiet, that I preferred Roberta Flack to B.B. King. I was a reader, and I wanted to become a writer, but when I tried to write original stories I found that words and their meanings can be elusive, difficult to control, because they can move in every direction at once. I never knew where to begin. At which point does a story begin? The question is unanswerable because some relevant event, thought, or observation always predates the action. There can never be a total story, one that encompasses everything past, present, and future.

Music can reference the past by playing sounds from dated genres, and it can be played in different rhythms, at different tempos, and in different time signatures, but its articulation is always heard in present time. Writing is read in present time, but it can easily move among different times, from the past through the future. It can disappear into alternate timelines. For that reason, the form of writing that resonates with me most is memoir, a subgenre of fiction. A memoir can begin at any point. It can become a search for origins, or an excavation of memory. It can play double Dutch with time and memory, can illustrate how the past sometimes follows the future, and the present sometimes freezes in its advance.

~

I ran away from home at sixteen. Back then I still played the alto saxophone. I wasn't yet ready for the tenor, whose size and legacy intimidated me. I could physically encompass the alto, and that gave me confidence in my playing. I took my horn and busked downtown by Bay Street station. After several hours and an aching embouchure, I made enough money to buy a Greyhound ticket to Montréal. I didn't know anyone in Montréal, but I knew the city by reputation. I knew it from my French immersion program at school. It was the city of music, the contrary city of referendums and street protests, of bridge blockades and military incursions, of explosives detonated in the stock exchange. The news reported that landlords were desperately lowering rents to attract tenants. Everyone had left for Ontario after the referendum, and thousands of apartments were vacant. The idea to move in the opposite, contrary direction thrilled me. My parents expected me to focus on my future. I didn't want to think about the future. I wanted the past. I wanted cobbled streets, a derelict old city that inhaled cigarette smoke and exhaled art. I didn't care for real estate or early mornings. I moved opposite my classmates who loved pop music, sports, beer, and were comfortable in their parents' suburban basements. I wanted a small apartment downtown, its walls lined with books, its quaint front balcony overlooking a narrow street. Across the street, a café where I would sit with an espresso reading novels by Maryse Condé and Amos Tutuola. I wanted a rhythm section that included drums, upright bass, percussion, and keys. The percussion would include conga, quinto, tumbadora, as well as all of the gourds, rattles, and shakers that animate African music. The keys would ideally be an organ, but a piano would be welcome, as might a Rhodes, a Clavinet, or a Wurlitzer. I would provide voice and brass. I could scream, shout, speak, sing, or blow. That combination would allow me to reference most genres of Black music from Africa, the Caribbean, Latin America, and the States. I would need to find musicians whose vocabularies matched mine, and who could improvise freely. I thought I might find all of this in Montréal, as well as a reprieve from my parents, who were startled by my hair twisting into dreadlocks. That, for them, was cause for deep anxiety. What had they done to deserve a child who wanted dreadlocks? Daily they reminded me that the way I dressed would influence the way people treated me, so if I wore dreadlocks, people would assume I was "anti-establishment." I reminded my parents that Toronto wasn't Jamaica circa 1975, but they wouldn't hear it.

When I reached Montréal I busked outside Berri metro. I didn't know where else to go. I thought it would be best to make as much money as possible, so I played for a few hours, then took a break and followed a group of itinerant Ontario squeegee punks uptown to St-Louis Square. I managed to busk for a few more hours in Sherbrooke metro before the rush-hour crowds thinned. By then my lips ached, my cheeks were sore, and I was straining to hit notes in the middle of my register.

I packed my horn and wandered across St-Denis Street, where I noticed a box on the sidewalk. It was full of books. I stood by the box for a moment, expecting someone to rush up and claim it, but people passed and no one glanced at it. I rummaged. One of the books had a speckled gray cover with a yellow strip running down the middle, and the words: *Sur la route* printed along the yellow strip. I found another book that bore the image of a shirtless, muscled Black man holding a hatchet aloft, grimacing, and two wild dogs lunging toward him: *L'esclave vieil homme et le molosse*. I went into Lafleur, which smelled of grease and detergent, and I sat in one of its yellow booths. As I waited for my poutine I read—in a misdirected and halting fashion—through the jacket copy of both books. When I left the restaurant I dropped *Sur la route* back into the box.

I wandered the Plateau, noticing the red À LOUER signs in windows and the lilac bushes in full bloom. I swooned at the feeling of being in a European city with narrow streets, old stone buildings with stained glass and heavy wood double doors. I resolved that after another day's busking I would knock on some of those doors and offer to pay rent. Darkness fell slowly over the squat brick homes. The smell of lilacs drifted. Someone was practicing piano, and the ivory notes hung in the dusk. I returned to the park. Punks gathered by the fountain and drank beer. Some sang songs, others roughhoused with their dogs, and others snored on the benches after a day of squeegeeing. They were joined by college students who smoked joints and strummed guitars by the fountain. Some of them wandered back down to St-Denis and Sherbrooke to make a few extra dollars.

The water from the fountain splashed down into a concrete pool. A drunk couple took off their shoes and sloshed through the pool laughing, picking up pennies, nickels, dimes. I crashed on the grass facing the 19th century sandstone homes, the ones in which the poet Émile Nelligan was rumored to have lived. The houses had once been majestic, but their paint was now curling, their balconies were eaten by wood rot and were home to families of squirrels, and their wrought iron railings were gnawed by rust. Around 5 o'clock in the morning two police cruisers pulled into the park. I heard gravel crunching, doors opening and slamming, and then yelling, scuffling. I grabbed my saxophone and ran out of the park. I hurried along Prince Arthur's cobblestones, and when I glanced back I saw people gesticulating, swearing, staggering under heavy backpacks and the twin burdens of morning and alcohol. The freedom of the previous night's celebrations had curdled. I bought a coffee in Café Dépôt, and washed my face and underarms in the washroom. I wandered St-Laurent. The windows of vacant businesses had been pasted over with posters for poetry slams and indie rock shows. Some of the posters hung in ribbons. Others were faded, but words like YAWP! still bulged forth. I eventually wandered to the business district, close to the river. I opened my case and stood with my back to the Maisonneuve monument, the one with the Iroquois man squatting near its base. I looked into his bronze eyes, then at his wiry figure crouched down. One of his hands was open, while the other curled around the handle of a hatchet. I touched his face, and that touch became a caress. I wanted to say something to him, but all I could think of was, *bonjour*.

I moistened the reed and fingered the keys absently. I held my breath before blowing anything. That silent second grew longer, and in its widening interval I felt myself falling.

~

In the darkness behind my eyes I faintly made out a rect-angular shape. I concentrated on the form, realizing that it was a house, a common stone structure like others along the rue Saint-Paul, which curved along the southeastern tip of the island. I had passed in and out of that house for years. I had scrubbed its wide floorboards, swept it, washed its windows, sweated in it. I belonged to it. I had cooked in its kitchen and hurried through its rooms every time the mistress, always irritable, called. The house belonged to the widow de Francheville, and it stood, dimly outlined against the night. I leaned back into a copse of trees, beyond which ran more of the broad, dirty streets of the port, and beyond that the Saint Pierre River, which followed the curve of the island and fed into the Saint Lawrence River.

As I stared at the house I held my breath. At any second flames might leap out from the widows and claw at the roof. I willed the flames to twist outside and stretch upward. I had been subject to the widow de Francheville's every demand, to her blows and curses, and I had deliberately placed hot coals on the wooden roof beams and blown on them until they glowed. As I stared at the house, I prayed for the widow's misery to burn hotter than the fire that would embrace her as she slept.

I had to reach the mouth of the Saint Pierre River, where a canoe was waiting. Once the flames surged above the house and cast sparks toward the moon, every single person from every neighboring home would rush outside, and if the wind blew in the right direction, those flames would be swept to the nearest rooftops and might ignite the entire port. What if they did? Did any of it belong to me?

I had not confided my plans to anyone. I had promised myself that if a fire were to break out in the night, as had happened before in the colony, I would lead the other enslaved people outside. I swore that I would not be moved by soft compassion. I would not wake any of the owners. I would pray for every slave owner in the port to be burned in their sleep. Again, I shuddered at the viciousness of my thought, the ease by which it appeared, and my ability to think it and feel justified in doing so.

As the flames soared, everyone who shared my color, who shared my bonded condition would be assembled, counted, and interrogated, and then it would be discovered that I was missing. There would be shouting, cursing, running—would there be concern for my life, or would the concern be more for the loss of property? Nobody would find me. Mastiffs imported from the plantations of the Antilles, from the îles à sucre, would be roused.

I looked up, and the moon pointed its clear silver finger down toward the river. I was standing in the square again, blowing. It was night, and my saxophone case was full of coins and small bills. That night I slept in the Central Bus Station on Berri Street, and the next morning I caught a 6 am Greyhound home.

~

There exists a hierarchy among touring musicians, and nowadays I am somewhere near its middle. When I occasionally get bumped to the upper middle, I find myself flying first class, with executives contemplating my threadbare jean jacket, my dreadlocks, and my King Super 20 Silversonic tenor saxophone. Someone always meets me at the airport, and depending on the budget and prestige of the festival, that person might be a volunteer driving their own Subaru, a festival employee pushing a rented black suv with tinted windows, or a professional driver wheeling a Lincoln Continental limousine. In the back seat, a PR person hands me a sealed envelope containing a few hundred dollars, pounds, lira, yen, euros, and lets me know that I can ask her for "anything."

I recognize that even the experience of customs and airport security, waylaying and biased as it can be, is a long way from what I saw on my first tours in the early 2000s, when I could only get bookings at small clubs in small cities across Canada. On one of my first tours I was invited to play loft venues and grassroots festivals across the country. The money was poor, often pass-the-hat at the end of the gig, and the accommodations were dormitories or collective houses shared by groups of artists, but since I had the bookings, I managed to secure travel funding from the Ontario Arts Council, about a thousand dollars. I bought a pair of Fluevogs and an open-ended Greyhound ticket.

I wanted freedom, and saw it as the endless deferral of return. To fly, to maroon, to run, I wanted to define my trajectory. I might have to constantly adjust my course, but in that adjustment was a musical application. I was learning to improvise freely, to cover vast sonic distance without returning to the techniques and passages that were most comfortable. I wanted the agitation of flight. Flight was distinct from discovery or conquest. Its core principle was movement.

My ear for the cyclic rhythms of Caribbean music challenged my desire for free movement. I came to understand that repetition did not mean stillness or limitation. A reggae riddim was most dynamic when it was most grounded, most sticky. Subtle variation defined the figures being repeated. How could I integrate flight with repetition, with return? In a way, the question became a cultural one: How to fuse an African-American musical sensibility with a Caribbean one, and how to enact that fusion in a Canadian context? I would need to create my own genre, and not be content to mimic the established vocabularies. Naturally, the solution lay with my thousand-dollar open-ended Greyhound pass and my traveling shoes.

～

One night I awoke somewhere in the vast darkness of Ontario. Out the window the sky hung navy. The bus hummed through a tree-lined corridor. No other lights sped toward us. Eventually we stopped at a generic strip mall, and two loggers boarded. They sat across the aisle and announced that they were brothers, reunited at their father's funeral after having been estranged for 20 years. One of them was carrying a paper shopping bag. When the other instructed him to "break out the loot," they snickered, opened the bag, and urged me to look inside. The bag was two-thirds full of miniature bottles of Smirnoff, Johnnie Walker, Chivas Regal, and Beefeater, which they poured into cans of Coke. One of them offered me his can. I declined, he insisted, and this continued until I pretended to be asleep. I listened to their low voices, their exclamations of "oh yah eh?" "Listen buddy!" Their muffled chuckles skittered down the aisle of the sleeping bus, "yaknowwhatImean?" "An then I told him I sez to him, I sez hey!" As they talked the smell of whiskey soured the air.

In an undergraduate history class we'd watched the NFB documentary *Speakers for the Dead*, about the town of Priceville, Ontario, initially settled by Blacks who fled US slavery. They cleared the land, erected homes, and raised families, yet when the government distributed deeds to the land, none of the Black settlers were granted deeds. They were forcibly displaced, sometimes in the middle of the night. Their homes were set afire, or they were confronted by chanting, torch-wielding mobs. They dispersed. Their aggressors stole possession of their homesteads. Priceville also maintained a "sundown law," which meant that any

Black person found lingering in town after sundown would suffer unspecified consequences. Shocked, I told my parents about the sundown laws, and they told me that some small Ontario towns kept those unofficial laws active into the 1980s. Failing to fall asleep on that midnight bus I wondered about the towns we passed, and about the snoring, reunited brothers, about whether they, their fathers, or their grandfathers might have enforced those laws.

~

I awoke in the night, deep in Southwestern Ontario. The bus had stopped at what seemed to be a strip mall, but I was fresh from a dream and still half-submerged in sleep, so all I remember is the Dunkin' Donuts. The night was cool and it felt like winter was invisibly crystalizing in the late autumn air. Inside, fluorescent lights buzzed over the depleted donut display case. Tina Turner's serrated voice cut through the speakers.

The shop was empty, save for a lone hippie, with long brown hair parted in the middle, sitting at a far table. He was wearing a green army surplus jacket, worn corduroy pants, and combat boots. A black guitar case was propped against the wall next to him, and the case was covered in stickers. A mug of coffee sat in front of him. Both he and the mug looked like they'd been there forever. His head was down and his hands were rolling tobacco from a pouch of Drum. The teenage girl behind the counter was pale, with near-white hair, white eyelashes, and tiny squinting eyes that were placed very close to her nose. Her lids seemed to flutter low over her eyes as she watched us shuffle, half dreaming, toward the register. I wanted to get out of that network of small, isolated towns as quickly as possible. I bought a muffin and a bottle of water. The girl at the register barely parted her lips when she spoke. Her teeth were small, rounded, and bright yellow.

~

I awoke and felt a presence. A young man was standing some feet away, against a wall of lockers, watching me. We made eye contact, then I looked down at my saxophone, my road case, my suitcase. They were all there. I looked back at him and he sneered, then circled away. He had on sagging jeans that were frayed at the cuffs, an oversized track jacket, a bandana beneath his baseball cap. He walked with a slight limp, and finally leaned up next to the men's washrooms. To my right a man snored at irregular intervals, then a placid expression spread over his face. As the expression spread, I noticed a dark stain spreading down his pant leg. It was three o'clock in the morning, and the other passengers were dispersed throughout the Brandon bus terminal, sitting on the hard, plastic seats, watching the departure gate for their cue to transfer to a new coach.

My hangover throbbed and parched me. All the way from Winnipeg I thought I was going to vomit, the motion of the bus and the stale air in the cabin making my stomach churn. As the bus rolled, long slow waves of nausea overcame me, then receded. After an hour the waves quickened, and the interval between them lessened. I got up and wove my way down the aisle to the washroom. It was like walking on snow, uncertain whether the next step would be solid or whether my foot would fall through fluff. The aisle jiggled. I bumped against the seats on either side. My stomach flipped and I clenched my teeth.

Directly ahead of me, in the rear row of seats, a man wearing a green US Army surplus jacket, a bandana around his hair, and mirror shades sat with his legs spread open. The aisle itself pointed directly between them. His brown corduroy pants were worn, and a guitar case lay on the seat next to him. It was covered in stickers: Barranquilla, Moose Jaw, Soweto, Savannah, Taber, Sydney, Quito, Peterborough. He sat immobile, and I couldn't tell whether he was sleeping or not. His shades reflected the seats and windows stretching down both sides of the aisle. In his shades I could see silhouettes of pine and spruce flashing past outside the bus, and beyond them, the night sky and the odd star glittering in the distance. If I looked close enough I might make out the Big Dipper, Orion, an owl spreading its wings and swooping down from a branch. As I looked into the reflection it seemed to expand, until I was no longer swaying down the aisle of the bus, but inside the reflection.

~

Above me were branches, and above them the night sky. Below me were branches as well. I was high enough up that the ground disappeared into darkness. I heard water rushing close by, and felt the cool air sweep over me, but even though I glanced down, I couldn't locate the water. I tried to shift to get more comfortable. My legs were sore, and I was squatting on a thick branch. I wasn't wearing a shirt, but I had on coarse cloth pants, and no shoes. My soles ached, but I was afraid to move. The wind rose again, and I thought of the word "nature," and how even though I'd worked outdoors since childhood, only now did the word mean something to me. It meant something immense and indifferent that concealed dogs, men on horseback with rifles, and the past, back to which the dogs and men wished to drag me, whereas I wanted to flee into the future. I did not know anything about the future save that it held eventual freedom. I had often heard people say that someday their children, or their children's children would be free, but I wanted it for myself. I knew that if I fled far enough into the future my freedom would be complete, and I knew that the future lay north. A bat twisted and zigzagged through the branches, and then another, and then another. I shivered amid a growing swarm of bats. Then I heard the dogs and men, and the swarm of bats grew more dense. They surrounded me like smoke, concealing me from my pursuers, never even grazing my bare skin. The intricate, crisscrossing lines of flight confused me, and made me think of handwriting, something I had always wanted to learn so that I too, like those slaves turned northern abolitionists, could write about my life in bondage and my escape. I knew that it might never happen, but I thought that someone else might hear of my story and write it down. I decided, then, in a low voice, to whisper it to the bats. The bats would carry it, in their vertiginous swoops and arcs, into the future. I understood then that the purpose of my life was to be a fugitive slave hiding in a tree at night, shivering inside of a book that hadn't yet been written. I closed my eyes and tried to imagine what the book would say. I spoke in a very low voice so nobody would hear me. I told my story to the bats and they wrote it in the branches before scattering.

~

I stumbled into the bathroom, locked the door, and vomited as quietly as I could. I breathed with my mouth open as my stomach heaved up into my throat again, and then I spat into the bowl, rinsed out my mouth, and wobbled back to my seat. The hippie was still sitting in the same position, obscured behind his shades. Night rushed alongside the bus. Night rushed into his depthless, parallel mirrors. I found my seat and sat suspended between sleep and waking, trying to block all thought from my mind and focus on an image of perfect opacity.

By the time my stomach settled we reached the Brandon terminal. I was in the middle of the prairies alone, sick, hoping that the next bus would arrive before the more desperate locals became too familiar. The bus station was a tiny lighted outpost plunged into the autumn as it descended toward winter. Young men circled, wandered outside to bum smokes, sat in corners sipping from bottles concealed in paper bags, or slept fitfully in the tight plastic chairs.

The prairie yawned. I knew that the people who spent nights prowling the bus station, who stared out from its streaked windows, who huddled against its walls sleeping, might disappear, just as the people who cleared land and built farms in the Ontario countryside, who spent nights awake listening to the forest rustle and buzz, long before the drone of electricity, had eventually been dispersed. Where had they gone? Who would know? Who would search for them? In a way, I was them. I was descended, somewhere along the branching line, from people who had disappeared.

I was on tour: improvising, adrift on the prairie, as I had been in 1791, or 1812. My tour consisted of me sitting alone in a bus station with alcohol in my blood, among others who were penniless and stranded, some of whom hustled the washrooms for enough to buy a ticket to Winnipeg, Weyburn, Moose Jaw, Portage la Prairie, Swift Current, Regina, Lloydminster, Red Deer, or Calgary. I stayed awake. I stared outside and waited for the Greyhound's headlights to puncture the dark.

~

The sunlight slid down my hotel window. I was in Fredericton for two concerts at the jazz festival. After that, my European tour would kick off in Zurich. I opened my eyes just long enough to take in the brilliant white bedclothes rumpled around me, the light suffusing the room, before letting fatigue draw my eyelids back down. My thoughts, which had momentarily broken the surface of a dream, were submerged again.

In the dream I was standing under a maple in the early morning. It was so early it was still dark, with dew gleaming like stars on the black leaves that hung overhead. The air was damp, and the scent of the river mixed with the freshness of morning. I worried that the glistening leaves were a dewy net suspended above me which, if I didn't escape it quickly enough, would collapse atop me, and as its dewdrops soaked into the earth, the net would pin me to the ground. But even though my heart leaped into my throat each time I heard a slight rustle, I couldn't leave from beneath the tree. A breeze rippled through its branches, and I froze.

I didn't know who, among the others who were bonded to the farm, would visit me. I knew to wait for them, as they would bring me a bundle of food scraps and old clothes, into which I could change after I crossed the river. The change of clothes would be valuable, because when the runaway notices began to appear in Fredericton, Halifax, Montréal, and other towns between, I would be identified as wearing clothes I'd already burned. I would have shed my skin, become a ghost among living men and women. Wasn't I already something like that? I waited under the glistening net, until I could push the canoe out into the river, and with the food and clothes in the bottom of the canoe, the cutlass across my lap, I would paddle to the opposite bank. The wet streak of moonlight hovering atop the river would serve as my guide.

I had often wondered how long a person could stay at large, could stay hidden, when the world itself conspired to trap and return them. I wondered how a person who could be so insulted and beaten, whose life seemed worth nothing, could suddenly be of great value once they no longer belonged to anyone. The notices would be up anywhere people gathered, with different sizes of lettering alternately speaking and shouting out from the page:

Fredericton, N.B. June 03, 1816

TWELVE DOLLARS REWARD

RUN AWAY from the Subscriber. On the night of June 01, a negro slave who answers to the name POMPADOUR, about 30 years, five and a half feet high, of copper color and tolerable appearance, with broad face and large lips, took with him a Canoe with Oars and Cutlass. Is...

I sat up and shielded my eyes against the Maritime sunlight. It was a Sunday. The final shows of the festival were that night, and the next morning we would all board planes. My next stops would be Zurich, Munich, Prague, Berlin, Hamburg, Amsterdam, Cologne, Brussels, Paris, where I would take a week to rest and experience the city before delving south to Barcelona, Madrid, and Lisbon. After that I would be free, with time stretching out before me like an open plain, money in my pocket and no return ticket bought, no itinerary dividing my hours. I could languish there in Lisbon by the ocean, reading about the decline of grand slaveholding families like the Londônias-Figueiras in Brazil, and contemplate venturing south to Gibraltar, Casablanca, and Marrakech, where I would hear the call to prayer rising up out of the mosques and hovering in the hot air, its sound crackling with earthiness and devotion, soaring out of the world of things and petty preoccupations. I could model my next record on the intonation of the call to prayer, or maybe not. I could fly straight to Dakar, perched far out on the vast Atlantic, with the Cape Verde islands, home to the great vocalist Cesária Évora, floating in the distant shimmer of my African gaze.

The festival staff told us that downtown Fredericton would be empty. Everyone was in church. The only alternative was the hotel brunch with its seven-dollar glasses of orange juice and its tourist families, which didn't bother me, but which the other artists wanted to avoid in favor of something more down to earth, more local, something that might include the words "stone-ground" and "artisanal."

Every shop, restaurant, café was closed. The streets were empty, and their emptiness added to their quaintness: 19th-century brick buildings, a cobbled square, a fountain, and the Maritime sky providing a postcard backdrop. It felt like Fredericton was posed, on its best behavior for us alone. The air was damp and tinged with a briny smell, which I might have been imagining, and I further imagined a thin layer of moisture from the Saint John River, or from the Bay of Fundy further south, teasing my skin. The idea was pleasant, and I thought of how nice it would be to return to Fredericton when the tour was over and find a place to rent, a few weeks in a riverside town... or I could buy a small house, one that I could visit twice a year just to escape Toronto and to work on ideas... I couldn't afford anything beyond a studio in Toronto, but in Fredericton? This was something to consider. I could even establish my own school of music, or start a small festival—why not do both?—and thereby become a fixture in the Maritime musical economy.

As we meandered, we passed a bar and grill that looked like it was open for breakfast. It had a large, open main floor with a bar in the center, and wooden steps up to a second-floor terrace where people could sit and overlook the main. The restaurant was empty save for one dejected hippie with a guitar case covered in stickers: Quito, Düsseldorf, São Paulo, Rhode Island, Edinburgh, Texas, Tijuana, North Battleford, Madrid. His stringy brown hair fell over his shoulders. The treads of his brown corduroys were worn nearly flat, and he was hunched over a mug of coffee that looked like it long ago went cold. A pouch of Drum sat on the table in front of him, and he was absorbed in the act of rolling cigarettes.

The place smelled like an army surplus shop, a mixture of mold, sweat, and old tobacco. All of the chairs, tables, and silverware seemed left in place from the last setting. Even the hippie seemed like he had been there forever, slowly rolling his cigarettes and ignoring his cold coffee. Time had stopped, and for a moment we stood staring into the big empty room, watching the dust hover. A gray-haired figure materialized in a beam of light. He shuffled toward us. He placed his hands on his hips and disinterestedly offered, "what do youse need?"

I rolled my eyes and was about to urge the group to find another place when one of the musicians chirped, "We're here for the breakfast."

The older man sighed, "I'll need to see some ID." I thought this a strange request, but the others dug out their wallets and extracted cards. The owner ignored their cards and raised a finger toward me, "I need to see yours."

In any similar situation I might offer a rebuke, but among my newfound international friends, happy to be in a restaurant that served some local flavor, I obliged. I handed him my drivers' license. He held onto it and circled behind the bar. He reached under the bar for a pair of spectacles, perched them low on his nose, and examined my license. "Toronto, eh." He smirked.

He kept staring at the license, and just as I was about to ask him what he was doing, one of my companions asked, "Don't you want to see our ID?"

Another echoed, "Yeah, don't you want to look at our ID?" I was older than all of them. I was the only one with gray hair. I was the only one with eyes that looked tired from touring and from struggling to discover ways to express things I didn't want to confront, but that I had to get out somehow, that I had to share and examine publicly.

I took a step toward the bar. "Excuse me—"

He pulled back and declared, "I don't see a birthdate on this license." He turned the license toward me, as if it were an exhibit in court. "Where is it?"

I pointed to the birthdate and slowly recited the numbers, "Nineteen, zero-six, one-nine-eight-zero. Nineteenth June nineteen-eighty. That's the birthdate."

He squinted at the license, shook his head slowly, and concluded, "I'm inclined to believe this isn't a legitimate drivers' license, and as a citizen upholding of the law, I am required to confiscate it." He then looked at me over the rim of his spectacles.

I snatched the thin plastic card from between his thumb and index, and I blurted, "No you won't."

He continued staring over the rim of his spectacles, still with his index and thumb pressed together, no longer separated by the thin plastic. He blinked, as if his mind was only slowly registering what had happened. I took a step back, and gave my friends a look that said, through a combination of wide eyes and pursed lips, "Let's go. Now." But they only stared back.

"Get out." His eyes took us all in, then he raised his voice. "Get out or I'll call the cops."

My friends surged forward at this, pointing and arguing, "This is outrageous."

"We have just as much right to be here as anyone else."

"You can't tell us to leave."

His hands darted under the bar. He bent down for a second, and in that second I managed to utter, "Let's go," before he sprang back up shaking a Louisville Slugger so old its wood was the color of ash. His other hand held a matte black rotary phone, which he slammed on the bar, shouting, "Get out! Get the hell out of my bar!"

We backed out, and I took a final glance into the room. It was empty. The sunlight slanted through the windows on one side of the building, and dust floated in the angled light. The hippie hadn't moved. He hadn't even glanced up.

Instinctively we turned back toward the hotel, and my friends erupted, indignant, "We can't let him do that."

"We shouldn't let him get away with that. We need to tell somebody."

"We need to go back in and confront him."

I told them to forget it and keep walking. I wanted to tell them to shut up and stop acting like children. I wanted to remind them of our location, in a tiny town perched on the eastern edge of the country, where we didn't have a single blood relative.

They walked, but they kept looking over their shoulders. The owner was now outside staring after us. I looked back just as he raised his ashen bat and shouted. His voice reached us, but the words it carried were indistinct. "Ignore him," I said, "He's just an old fool," but I knew he wasn't exactly a fool. He was a man who knew what he wanted. For a few blocks my companions wouldn't let it go. They were charged by the shouting and the explosion of rage and bitterness, yet they seemed unable to contextualize what they just witnessed, as if stunned by the confirmation that such a thing had materialized in their lives. I stayed quiet, and after a few blocks their ire turned inward and smoldered in silence. We continued to the hotel and I focused on omelettes, espresso, arugula salads, and vegetarian sausages.

When the young hostess beamed and welcomed us, I relaxed. She led us to a booth by the window. The morning sun glazed our table, and with the warmth and brilliance everyone's cheer returned. The restaurant grew busy, and childrens' voices bubbled. Conversations carried through the room, and as I listened to the fragments I thought of bringing a recording device—a Zoom—into a busy restaurant and recording the ambient noise and using that as a sonic backdrop for an extended improvisation. But then I thought, no. Invite a dozen people into the studio and prepare a script, with all sorts of intolerant language—continuous streams of invective against Niggers and Chinks, Pakis and Wetbacks, found phrases from *Globe and Mail* columnists, from the *Journal de Montréal*, quotes from Conservative and Reform politicians deriding multiculturalism and diversity, attacks on the idea of immigration, rants by Vancouver suburbanites hysterical about their own children becoming minorities in their own neighborhoods and themselves being priced out of the real-estate market by wealthy Chinese, and have everyone speak those texts at once. Then—then, I would use that as the sonic backdrop for a furious, screeching, micro-tonal noise improvisation on our national anthem. It was a terrible idea, but I was enjoying thinking about it while lightly peppering my asparagus and goat cheese omelette.

"I mean, I hate to say this, but I am a little disappointed." It was the American, a woman from New York who was playing piano, organ, and electronics as part of the supporting group for the son of a legendary jazz musician. When we first met we bonded over gear-talk: clocking devices and random voltage sources for our modular synthesizers. She drew brown hair away from her angular face and said, "I guess I'm just disappointed that you didn't want to stay and fight." I sighed and put down my fork.

"If you want to fight it so badly, then why don't you? Why don't you get up and leave your nice brunch here, and go back to that bar and fight the injustice? Don't let him get away with it."

She looked to the other two for support, but one was intently focused on the empty street outside the hotel, and the other was efficiently moving food from one hemisphere of his plate to the other. Her face fell, and her eyes searched a pile of fried potatoes, seasoned with fresh rosemary and smoked paprika, for an answer.

~

I was hired to play Caribana in Toronto, as part of a horn section on one of the large floats that rolled slowly down by Harbourfront, blasting soca music. While I do love old-time calypso bands, I don't like soca music. Unlike reggae, its repetition doesn't contain subtle shifts and improvised riffs. Its point is its relentlessness, its rhythmic bludgeoning, and only through prolonged exposure at high volumes do I internalize its groove, at which point all kinds of space opens up within the tempo. But I can't tolerate it for that long. Soca is exclusively for the body, whereas I also listen for ideas, for liberation of thought. And then there is the performance of soca, the hoarse-shouted commands to *jump an wave, wine yu waist*, repeated ad infinitum. To accompany that, my carnival costume was black short-shorts and a red sequined top, with glitter smeared on my thighs, arms, and cheeks. I was more underdressed than I had ever been in public, and representing Trinidad and Tobago, even though my roots are in Jamaica and St. Vincent. It was incongruous, but the gig paid a few hundred dollars, and I was partly motivated to reorient myself to Caribbean music, beginning with the music I liked least, so I found myself on the float, half-undressed, smeared with glitter, punctuating a relentless soca riddim with horn hits, bored out of my mind and deafened by the volume, the bass from the subwoofers churning and thickening the summer air, and me feeling like a fever was coming on. It's possible I had sunstroke, or I was just overheated, overtired, or overexposed to the soca, but everything slowed down, a temporal melt. I let my horn dangle down and leaned back against the vibrating speaker. The crowd became a frenzied abstract painting, everyone a blur of movement and sound. In that smear of agitation in which no face was distinct, I noticed a boy. He was looking to his side and over his shoulder, anxious. At first I wondered whether he was lost, but then I realized he was an adolescent, with an inch-tall flat-top that faded down the back of his head. He was too old to be lost, I thought, as he glanced over his shoulder again and ducked past a group of women shaking their bodies and waving small island flags in time to the music. The boy dashed past two men, glanced back, and then kept zigzagging through the crowd. It seemed like the blurred crowd was moving faster than him. He wasn't blurred, he was clear and his movements were much more deliberate, like he was being pursued. His head turned toward the float and we locked eyes for a second. He looked away and dipped behind a person, and the float moved along, and then I saw a cop pushing through the crowd, pushing against the stream of people, and another behind her. They looked over and past people, and they were frantic. I looked for the boy again, but couldn't find him. As the soca riddim pounded I decided to improvise overtop, play something that would confuse the officers and speed the boy along. I blew as loud as I could; as I blew I imagined the officers losing their direction, running in circles, bumping into the parade-goers and getting accidentally smeared with glitter, while the boy continued zigzagging through the crowd, dashing against its current with agility and ease.

～

The last time I flew to Jamaica to play a music festival held in the island's second hottest parish, St. Elizabeth's, I spent my first two days in Kingston before being driven across the island, up the switchbacks through hills that rose into walls of jungle green. The green lolled in the heat, exceeded itself, tumbled down toward the ocean as if it wanted to dive into the water and escape the island. It was interrupted here and there by white-, peach-, or apricot-colored villas, homes with solid roman columns and verandas, clay roof tiles and elaborate wrought-iron grilles on the windows and doors.

The heat is more than just a feature of the region's climate. It is a vegetal entity, a being whose various moods sprawl, and whose presence you must navigate every moment of the day. The heat is not just the dry flare of the sun, but the humidity that steams off the earth and thickens the air. Although I am familiar with it, although it ignites a blood understanding the moment I step down the wheeled staircase and onto the ramp, it still dizzies me, slows my thinking.

At the airport I'd picked up a copy of the *Jamaica Journal*, because the entire issue commemorated the 150th anniversary of the Morant Bay Uprising. I had heard of Paul Bogle in reggae songs, and I knew that the uprising happened in the 1860s, after emancipation, but beyond that I didn't know any specifics. My first two days in Kingston

I was lethargic from the heat and jet lag. I slept and read in an air-conditioned condominium in a neighborhood that bore a Taíno name for iguana: *Liguanea*, and by the third day, when I was scheduled to be driven out to St. Elizabeth's, images of Paul Bogle's doomed march to the courthouse on October 11, 1865, and the indiscriminate slaughter of hundreds of people, the burning of over one thousand homes, surged in my thoughts. I knew that I had to express everything I was seeing in sound, that the tension and indignation that preceded the peaceful march needed to become terse statements that stretched into melodic passages that would reference the classic reggae devotional Satta Amassagana. They would repeat and be improvised upon, and they would be gradually subsumed by increasing rhythmic intensity, one that would nearly fly apart with velocity and noise, but would transcend itself and finally take flight on dirge-like gospel chords, and then hymn itself into silence. I wanted Paul Bogle's march to the courthouse to be the score that I would interpret. I thought that my two bare feet could provide the rhythm, that of "my feet is my only carriage," of walking along a country road, a steadiness, against which the increasing tempo of my horn playing would strain. I had an ankle-bangle that I had never worn before, but that I'd bought in an African boutique in Peel metro in Montréal. It was an exquisite work, and the vendor swore it was direct from Senegal. It was a black iron band, which slipped over the foot and rested below the ankle, and small wrought-iron elephants dangled from it. Each elephant contained an iron ball that jangled inside its body whenever the band was shaken.

I couldn't play my horn in the air-conditioned condo-minium, so I lay back on my bed with the horn in my hands, no mouthpiece attached, closed my eyes, and visualized myself playing the work. I fingered the notes I heard in my head. I counted two different tempos, one for my feet and another for my hands and breath. In this fashion I refined my ideas. I decided to title the piece "Morant Bay Hosanna," and I repeated the title to myself as I paced the condo wait-ing for my ride.

Kingston's concrete walls, buildings, billboards, and traffic thinned as we left the city behind. Its dustiness, its pale brown backdrop was gradually fleshed with green. The highways widened. The heat fell upon the countryside in long supple waves. I looked out at the expanse of fields, and I wondered how much the country's landscape had changed in the 150 years since the uprising.

~

I was first introduced to the idea of being a touring musician by TV commercials for Stompin' Tom Connors. They aired on the Canadian channels in the evenings, and they featured footage of Tom, a hardscrabble folk musician, leading what I assumed to be a rowdy Alberta bar crowd in a chorus about "the good old hockey game". There was humor in the delivery, but also self-mockery. I tried to imagine how it felt to play for a beer-drinking audience, to people who appeared to mock the songs by shouting the chorus, to mock the author. Perhaps Tom had once aspired to be an artist, but had been reduced by a parochial country that only understood art as something to drink, stomp, and shout along to. I hated the entire schtick, but I was fascinated. I knew that musicians toured, played sold-out arena shows in big cities, but I didn't know anything about a more common, more local variation on touring. I never thought that a person could "tour Canada." I grew up believing that Canada was essentially four cities: Toronto, Montréal, Ottawa, and either Vancouver or Halifax, depending on your coastal orientation, and those major cities were stitched together by churches, farms, small towns, by a thin thread of lonely humanity, immigration, industry, and ignorance. Unless a person had family in one of those small towns, I never understood why anyone would deliberately visit. Entrenched in my Caribbean Toronto bias, I believed in a narrative of progress, which assumed that small towns were meant to be left behind.

I imagined that Tom never slept indoors, that he was comfortable cozying up to a smooth rock, tilting his cowboy hat down over his face, and drifting off under the prairie sky with his guitar by his side. I pictured the stars fixed in place above him, and as he dreamed of lions and scorpions, quivers of arrows, and mythical heroes, a coyote howled in the distance.

On the other hand, I am not a rustic. I'm also not a folk musician, although I often think about Charles Mingus's assertion that jazz is Black people's folk music. I half-agree. First, I'd say that the Black folk he is talking about are the ones with roots in the United States. Second, I'd say that jazz issues from the blues and gospel, and that it maintains a relationship with soul and funk, but that it can travel beyond folk forms. If I were to define a folk form, I'd say: a music that articulates the concerns of a particular people in their vernacular. "Concerns" doesn't have to mean social conditions. It can also mean feelings, dreams, or fantasies. Jazz sometimes travels outside the realm of vernacular and common understanding. Whether to its detriment or its advantage, it can be purely academic. It can distance itself from its folk origins, as a person who is born on a farm can distance themselves from the land, can ascend to a penthouse overlooking Toronto with a fridge full of truffles, champagne, and prosciutto.

But then again not everyone will achieve—or will even want to achieve—that ascent. For some, the ascent is punishment, and even a slight distance of a foot or two from the earth might become an impossible distance. In the National Gallery of Jamaica, downtown Kingston by the waterfront, I saw a small painting, which reflected the time when slavery was active on the island. An African man had his flank pierced by an iron hook, which hooked around one rib, and poked out the flesh below. The man's hands were bound behind his back, his feet were bound, and the hook was attached to a short chain, which was affixed to a gibbet, and the contraption raised the man one foot off the ground. He hung twisted, doubled over, and blood dripped to the ground, and on the ground beneath him were bleached skulls, several perched atop pikes around the gibbet, as if to preclude any imagination but depravity and violence, and to expose it in the dry glare of the sun. The man hung there, wide-eyed, roasting. I stared into his eyes and I could not fathom the extent of his suffering, how every second must have contained an intolerable, sweltering eternity, how he looked back into my eyes without blinking, and his look let me know that his suffering was eternal, and that it encompassed my visit to the island, my existence, and that of the world. As he turned on his iron hook, the ships docked and unloaded their human cargo, the sugar estates roared to life, the enslaved marooned and disappeared into the green of the Blue Mountains, the plantations fell derelict, the ships stopped arriving, Kingston swelled, the airlines soared with their cargo of emigrants, the blue plastic barrels were shipped home, families were separated and reunited in Miami, New York, or Toronto, and the emigrants returned to the island to visit family, wearing loud jewelry and bearing gifts for everyone, and still he turned on his hook and stared forth. On many days he didn't see anyone as he stared into the quiet of the gallery, and on those days he suffered the longest. The room was air conditioned, but in his painting, where he lived as he died, it was always midday. The empty nights in the dark of the gallery were quiet, but the sun always blazed inside his frame. Sometimes a security guard would walk over and inspect him, hanging there in the painting, with his eyes never closing, his eyes open all day and all night, and the security guard would groan, or sigh, and then would continue on his rounds through the building. On other days when the gallery was full, the hanging man would twist on his hook and stare out at the tourists with their groomed dreadlocks, their glowing skin, their dark gold bracelets, and he would understand their desire to connect with their history, and their total distance from it, their horror at the idea of stepping out of their present and into the documentary painting with him.

~

My hotel room in Kingston, Ontario, overlooked Lake Ontario. In one direction, the lake widened toward the horizon. In the other, it narrowed into the Saint Lawrence river, which flowed toward Montréal. I had the night off, and was sitting in a bathrobe staring out to the dock and the lake, to a few boats in the distance, and to some small human figures walking by the waterside. The entire hotel, even the city, floated atop Lake Ontario, and I liked that sense of being adrift in the night with the stars in the distance. Was this how Stompin' Tom felt when he was alone on the prairies, traveling from one bar show in Red Deer to another in Moose Jaw? Was this what those rural blues musicians felt as they migrated north to Chicago? That sense of drift is why I like extended forms, because drift can't be contained in a three-minute song.

Stompin' Tom decided to contain his entire career within Canada. Perhaps this is his folk inheritance as well, because the music loses its immediate references the farther it travels. What of Sonny Boy Williamson in London, Mahalia Jackson or Memphis Slim in Paris? Stompin' Tom's focus was the national and the local, and that's admirable, but it's impossible to duplicate. I am pulled in too many directions. Sometimes I feel like I'm being pulled apart. That's why I like Kingston, this little strained junction between Canada and Québec. It feels like the most ambivalent place in Canada because it is right on the lake, which becomes the *Fleuve St-Laurent*, which flows northeastward, past Montréal and out to the Atlantic, and then it spreads and deepens into the wider world. Lying there, adrift on my hotel bed, I felt I could fall asleep to the rocking of Lake Ontario, which is really the Saint Lawrence, which is really the Atlantic Ocean, which is really the world, which is what I am always attuned to, which is what I heard in the album that I had on repeat, Charles Mingus's *Cumbia and Jazz Fusion*, with the sounds of birds and insects mingling among the Latin rhythms. Mingus's bass, whose notes can drop with such density and weight, solidifies the undertone, and gives the work a groaning, oceanic rock.

I was adrift. I could wake up somewhere in the middle of the Atlantic Ocean, perhaps at the bottom of the ocean, walking barefoot along the ocean floor playing my saxophone, never having to remove my mouth from the reed to take a breath, just constantly blowing. As I blew and worked the keys, the groaning of the ocean changed its pitch, and an endless supply of air escaped my horn and ascended to the surface in a column, a vast bubbling column that parted the water. As the water parted, the skeletons of those who made the middle passage but who were thrown overboard, the cargo that died in the hold, or that fell ill yet survived in a fevered limbo, the human liabilities, as the captain, the traders, and the underwriters might consider them, the skeletons of those people drifted up from their bed in the ocean floor and drifted limply into the column of air, hundreds of them rushed into the column. The column foamed more furiously as it ascended, as it divided the tons of water, and the ghostly skeletons rushed to the surface as I blew, and I realized that I couldn't stop blowing until they had all entered the column, so I kept blowing and I didn't know how many there were, but they kept rushing into the column, and then my breath started to shorten. It shortened and shortened, and I strained against it, blowing from the bottom of my lungs, summoning air from the pit of my stomach, from my knees, finding hidden pockets in the muscles of my thighs, and further down between my toes, which had sunk into the sand. I blew all of the air out of my body, until my skin was sucked tight against me. I kept straining, and was suddenly wrung dry as the saxophone let out a final squeal and the final skeleton slipped into the stream of air, and rose up out of the ocean and into the sky, and the column faded, and I was breathless and afloat on the ocean in my hotel bed, in my bathrobe, staring out at the stars over the water, and I knew that all of those unnumbered dead at the bottom of the ocean had each found their stars, whose luminescence their life-force would power forever.

∼

I'm not from the prairies. I'm a stereotypical Easterner with immigrant parents from the Caribbean. Growing up, we took one of two trips each year: to Brooklyn, to visit my mother's family; or to Kingstown, St. Vincent, to visit my father's. Until the age of 30, I never ventured west of Ontario.

Before my most recent tour, which started in Western Canada, I was invited to contribute to a panel at Montréal's Blue Metropolis Literary Festival. It was an unusual invitation. The subject of the panel was the various intersections between music and literature. The organizers felt that my music displays "narrative qualities." I was flattered by that recognition, because my music addresses themes of distance and dispersal, and I treat the tenor saxophone as a voice, albeit a brazen, disembodied one. I think of the passages I play as being reflective of human passages, and being articulate in a way that recalls, or that calls out to language.

The panel featured musicians who had written novels, songwriters who wrote elaborate lyrics in the *chanson française* tradition, and poets whose work drew from musical forms. The sound poet Kaie Kellough, who is originally from Calgary, was on the panel. He was working on a collection of narrative essays about incidents he'd experienced on tour. He emphasized that not every tour stop can be Toronto or Montréal, and that in smaller cities you are forced to reckon with a culture that may not include, or understand, or accept you. His hair was sculpted into a tall gray mohawk that was twisting up into dreadlocks.

Standing outside the Edmonton airport I looked at my reflection in a window. I thought about that panel as I smoked, waiting for my ride. I looked tired. My locks were graying. Earlier, as the plane descended I looked down at brown, yellow, and green rectangles of land, at long sinuous expressways snaking to and from the city center, at tiny cars dotting the roads, and I instinctively thought, "I'm in another country."

I noticed people noticing me, with my saxophone slung over one shoulder, my suitcase and road case standing next to me. In Toronto I would blend in. I am an urban child, raised on the edges of Kensington Market. I imagined I was at the corner of Spadina and College on a Saturday in the summer with the streetcars passing and the Chinatown bustle jamming the sidewalks, reggae music pouring warm from a storefront speaker, neon images of fish and dragons lighting up windows, and people speaking in Cantonese and Mandarin as they passed. There I was, contemplating whether I should dip through the market to buy a patty and a ginger beer. I crave Caribbean food when I'm on tour, when I'm in constant drift between cities, between appearances, perhaps even between selves. I never arrive. The plane may land and my feet may touch the ground, but I don't spend enough time anywhere to become tethered by gravity, or by local experience. That sense of permanent suspension is the embodiment of diasporan ambivalence. It is also reminiscent of music. It takes off from silence, soars through sound, where it really resides, and temporarily lands in silence before resuming its journey.

Kaie recounted that he was once invited to Québec City to perform at a poetry festival. At the venue he noticed a table at which four men, all with Brylcreemed hair, long beards, flannel shirts, jeans turned up at the cuff, sat drinking pitchers of beer. When Kaie arrived they watched him.

"Every time I stood up to go to the washroom, to order an espresso at the bar, to greet the festival organizers, I drew their eyes. They were stern and twitchy, like dogs. I learned to become wary of expressions like theirs growing up in Calgary. I reminded myself that my face was on the promotional material for the festival, which was distributed throughout the city, so it's possible they recognized me. But if they did recognize me they didn't seem pleased about it.

"Maybe they were wondering if I was gay, or they didn't like my haircut, or they didn't like my clothes, bohemian stripes, loafers, and slacks. Perhaps it was a combination of all of those things. Maybe they didn't like the geometric patterns on my socks, or they objected to my posture, or to the way I held my head in the air. That's my attitude, and it's in the way I walk, the way I dress, the way I lean up against the bar and watch the room. And you know what? The good old boys in those smaller cities aren't used to seeing that confidence on a person like me. It unsettles them. Now, if you were a writer, how would you develop that narrative?" Kaie leaned forward, as if waiting for an answer.

"These are the interactions that some of us have at the intersection of literature and music. When I write about these episodes, which are everyday human experiences, it's very difficult to find the correct approach. Race is not something I've superimposed on the story. It is embedded in the experience, and I want a reader to understand that, but most readers will fixate on it. They will read it as if it rested on the surface of the narrative, even though it might reside deeper in the mix. One question I always ask myself is whether I should be less explicit, whether I should submerge mention of r—."

I understand what Kaie is saying, although he benefits from being a middle-class light-skinned man, and while he claims Guyanese heritage I've heard him say that he's more Canadian than he likes to admit. To his credit he's aware of his contradictions, but even so, people like him become indignant at the slightest suggestion of adversity because they've never known it deeply. I imagine that like many middle-class people, his importance has been reinforced. He's been told that he's somebody, that he has a voice and that it should be heard. Not all of us are sung that same refrain, and not all of us are driven by those same expectations.

I appreciate that he's forthright about race, which must be difficult to approach in writing. Instrumental music is abstract, so the idea of race is constructed by listeners based on the sounds they hear. Any musician can Blacken their sound, but nouns are explicit. They are specific and affixing. Once a noun has been deployed, it can't be called back. The only option is to send another noun after it, and then another, and another. There are always more nouns to deploy, more distinctions to make. A writer like Kaie has to write through race, an expression that I like because it seems to offer hope of an eventual emergence. But I don't think anyone ever emerges from race, certainly not a Black writer.

"Through dinner and through the event, as the poets were introduced and applauded, these guys drank pitcher after pitcher. Every time I glanced over they seemed to be looking at me. I wondered what their problem was. I realized it was me. I was their problem. These thoughts were confirmed a little later when, after a polite introduction and some applause, one of them rose up with a book in his hand and made his way to the stage. He read several poems in a deep, sonorous voice. His final poem was a rousing lyric with nationalist overtones, with a repeating figure that introduced each stanza: *le pays de*.... the country of... and each time that phrase was uttered it launched a declamation about farmers, people in canoes, people who tapped maple trees and wore beavers on their heads, explorers who piloted ships, and so on. As he repeated the anchoring phrase, he built momentum and drove a gradual crescendo. Two-thirds into the poem, his voice resonant and trembling with emotion, he stumbled. His momentum faltered.

"As he faltered he glanced at me, a single stolen glance in that speechless moment. We made eye-contact, and then his eyes darted away."

I finish my cigarette and stub it out as a black SUV pulls up. A middle-aged Edmontonian hops out. He's wearing a cowboy hat and an Oilers jersey. I extend my hand.

"Howdy," he says, extending his.

~

I encountered Kerouac in my teens. I found a copy of *The Dharma Bums* on a friend's bookshelf. I was briefly intrigued by the juxtaposition of the language of enlightenment with that of destitution. I randomly flipped through the book, and landed on a passage couched in an approximation of 1950s hipster slang, a fantasy of bohemian seediness mingling with African American culture. Bird—or someone reminiscent of Bird—blew like a spent angel, etc. etc. in the background. The narrator was trying to buy marijuana in the bathroom of a jazz club, and either the money, the drugs, or both items fell on the floor.

Fifteen years later I was given *On the Road* by an American musician I met at a festival in Fredericton, or Halifax.

He raved about it and said that Kerouac's writing moved like jazz improvisation. I decided to take the musician's word and give the book a chance. The idea that Dean Moriarty and the narrator had free passage wherever they wanted—across various states going east to west and returning, going south into Mexico, that they sped across the country as if they owned it, was disappointing. I wanted the narrator and Dean Moriarty to experience limitation, real life, to attempt to cross a border that they could not cross.

I wanted them denied passage precisely there where they desired it, or expected it most. Perhaps they would decide to go thrill-seeking in Harlem, where they anticipated scoring dope and losing themselves in jazz. But maybe they would get hustled, or carjacked by young undocumented workers up from Barbados. The narrator and Dean Moriarty would suffer a beating, and would be forced to flee on foot, to reckon with the idea that places exist where they are not welcome, where they are not entitled to free passage. Their narrative would be suspended, like shoes tossed over a wire.

The carjackers would joyride through the night, blasting Duke Ellington's *Blues in Orbit* and counting the money they stole from the interlopers, until the next morning when they would sell the car and purchase musical instruments, new suits, and luxury passage on a steamer bound for West Africa. On the steamer they would befriend the house band, a mix of artists from Nigeria, Harlem, and Ghana. The men from Barbados would jam with the band, adding their own distinct West-Indian inflection to the sound, and would create a novel global fusion that would transform music. The band would found a devotional temple in Freetown, Sierra Leone, in homage to the 600 Jamaican Maroons who were shipped from Nova Scotia to Freetown in 1800. The band would name its temple the Church of the Eternal Return, to which music lovers would flock to hear and be healed by the sound. Sixty-five years later I would arrive at the doorstep of the Church, on my first trip to the continent.

~

I caught a cab from the Winnipeg airport to my flat for the week, close to the Osborne Village. The back seat was separated from the drivers' seat by a thick plastic barrier, one that could withstand a battering of fists, the thrust of a blade, perhaps even a bullet. The city looked gray and white, blasted by cold and salt, and the news announced a polar vortex, which the cab driver echoed. He turned down the radio and told me the temperature would descend to minus 50. He whistled through his mustache and instructed me to go outside at night just to feel it, then added that winter didn't exist in Trinidad. He turned the radio back up as it announced that Regina would be even colder, 67 degrees below zero, which was colder than the surface of Mars. He whistled again, and I instinctively held my saxophone closer to my body. It's an instrument that seems to radiate heat, because the tenor saxophone can sound so close to the human voice, but also because its brass, even when tarnished, seems to glow from within, inhabited by fire and warmth. I need that warmth. I need to carry something reminiscent of that fire whenever I tour this country. It's not just a reminder of warmer climes, the saxophone, but of figures like Tituba and Mackandal, Cuffy and Quamina.

Quamina was born in Ghana, approximately 1778. At the age of 45, half a world from his birthplace, Quamina was involved in the Demerara Rebellion of 1823. He is now a national hero of Guyana. He possessed that remarkable resilience that enables a person to defy age, physical danger, humble origins, and social strictures, to shift the direction of the immovable world, to budge its revolution. I do not know whether I possess the same resilience. If I do, if there is any inside me, then that is what I summon in my live concerts; that is what I strive to disseminate. Archie Shepp called it Fire Music, and the Wailers called their sound Rebel Music, and I would agree with those taxonomies. I would add that my music thoroughly questions notions of sonic respectability, but that it also resists binaries like noise/melody, or improvised/written, vocal/instrumental, electronic/acoustic and the hierarchies that those binaries reify.

Critics used to accuse me of embracing difficulty for its own sake and of cultivating an abrasive sound, but on my last album I layered my sound into multi-instrumental compositions that took a melodic approach, and that alluded to—but never embodied—jazz standards like *Moanin'* and *Bye Bye Blackbird*, and the critics suddenly heard more in my sound; they were able to identify the lament of the blues, they said, and were able to situate me within the jazz tradition. The awards, accolades, *Downbeat*, *Fader*, *Jazz Times* profiles, and invitations followed.

The cab dropped me off at a squat brick building that looked more like a bunker fortified against the winter than a residence, but upstairs I was introduced to a spacious loft minimally decorated with restored teak furniture from the 1960s. The loft had a mezzanine and a rooftop terrace that overlooked the neighborhood. The loft belonged to one of the festival donors, the son of a national media baron, and he offered the luxury residence to the festival to house its featured performers. Framed black-and-white pictures of each feature performer hung on the exposed brick wall. Each performer was Black, and one of the conditions of my stay was that I would pose for just such a picture. Looking at the photos, I soured. I felt like he now owned these images. He had taken something of each of these artists. I would be next. I would be captured just like they had been, and something of me would forever hang in this room. I kept rehearsing ways of delaying the photo.

It was only six o'clock, but it was dark, and I stared out over the flatness and sprawl, the continuous unbroken trajectory crisscrossed by roads that disappeared into the prairie, the odd bus driving into the suburbs, its lights growing smaller and dimmer.

After a midnight spliff I decided to take my cab driver's advice. I bundled up, helped myself to an El Dorado Luxury Cask 25-year-old rum, then went outside onto the terrace to feel the cold. Staring out over the prairies (particularly for someone who grew up in the inner city) can inspire fear. The openness and flatness can feel desolate, and that sense of desolation is amplified by the wind that travels unimpeded across the landscape, shaping snow into drifts and scattering sound. I wondered how far a cry for help would travel across the prairie in the night, and whether the wind would catch and carry it to an ear, or disperse it immediately. I wondered how long it would take for my life force to ebb if I were walking along the highway, how far I would make it. I thought of Neil Stonechild, one of the boys that the Regina police drove out past the boundary of the city and dropped off in the snow. I choked on rum and tears and went back inside. I sat on the couch on the mezzanine, removed my saxophone from its case, which has become famous now that it's been photographed by jazz journalists, the case with the words **ROCKET NUMBER 9** stenciled in a military font along the side, and I blew air through the horn, producing just the faintest whisper that recalled the wind on the prairies, as I stared out at the flatness, the roads, the sky, the odd light in the distance, and thought of Neil Stonechild, and an idea for a continuously evolving melodic improvisation took shape.

The next morning, feeling numbed by the rum, I packed my road case with two semi-modular analog synthesizers that I would set to play in stereo, one playing ambient drones to evoke the flatness of the prairie, with a thin rustle of white noise to suggest something on the horizon, industry or inclement weather, and the other emitting low frequency pulses of varying lengths, to suggest the occasional tectonic buckle and swell. Atop that ambient pad I would play my horn, improvising the continuous melodies I'd fallen asleep thinking about. I tried to come up with a title and thought of "Stonechild Elegy." I called a cab and took my gear downstairs to the foyer.

The concierge was outside tossing salt on the walk, and it was a perfect prairie winter day, the kind where the sun is high and brilliant, the sky looks like a sheet of glass, and the snow is blinding. The concierge was squinting as he worked, his missing front teeth visible as his lip curled. Salt fell in slow arcs. I thought that the salt could be seeds of snow, seeds of winter being sown on the walk and he, the old sower of the season. He saw me standing in the foyer and he straightened. He squinted into the foyer, then put the bag of salt down and walked in.

"Good morning," I smiled, but he didn't reciprocate. He turned his back, then stomped the snow off his boots and looked outside. Once he finished stomping I continued, "I went outside late last night to feel the minus 50 temperatures. Something else!" He raised an eyebrow. In the silence of the foyer my words sounded stupid and obvious. He then walked up a step and stood directly behind me. I glanced over my shoulder. He stood barely a foot behind me with his arms crossed. He breathed.

I turned to the side so that he wasn't directly behind me. He glanced at me from under an ancient, battered Saskatchewan Wheat Pool cap. "Can I help you with something?" I asked. His lip curled again, and I worried that he might spit.

I picked up my horn and my road case and shifted to the opposite side of the foyer, so that if I looked to my right I could see him. His expression changed to something between a smile and a grimace. The words "do you have a problem" formed slowly in my mouth, but didn't get uttered.

He disappeared into the hall and a few seconds later

popped out from around the side of the building, staring straight into the foyer. He stood there looking at me for several minutes, and again I considered opening the door and asking him to explain his behavior, but decided against it. If he wanted to stand in the cold then he could, although he was probably immune to it. I wondered how immune he was, and how long he would last walking through the prairie night without his shoes, guided only by starlight.

We Free Kings

WHEN I READ THAT Delroy Portmore was murdered I wanted to scream, but instead I sobbed. No one else was home. My wife had taken our daughter to Surrey to visit her grandmother. It was a long drive from upper West Van to Surrey, so I had time. I felt guilty, as if I'd indulged myself, as if I'd done something I shouldn't do. My wife isn't demonstrative. She wouldn't know how to respond to my tears, and I pride myself on being collected, but the truth is that I still don't know myself. How many of us ever know ourselves, even when we have families, own homes, and manage careers.

Delroy Portmore was a Jamaican celebrity, a fashion designer to the dancehall superstars. He had 100,000 followers on Twitter, tens of thousands more on Instagram, and was interminably cresting on a wave of success. I'd never heard of him. He was in his thirties, graceful and dashing with long dreadlocks (which, I just read, he cut because the singer Beenie Man mimicked his way of styling them). He was beautiful, with the quality of dark skin that has an inner sheen, that always looks fresh because it has been nurtured by the equatorial humidity and the

Caribbean sun. I clicked through dozens of photos of him in dazzling kente-patterned suits, or posing in outré fashions that he'd designed, or grinning behind sunglasses with his dreadlocks assembled in a Little Richard style pompadour. The internet said that he had been the most prominent face of Jamaica's 2016 Pride celebrations, that he'd come out to his family, and that although it was difficult, they now supported him. And then I cried again, because I didn't know the circumstances of his murder, but I assumed it was hatred.

I browsed the articles in my Twitter feed. The *Jamaica Gleaner* advanced the angle of a domestic disturbance. Apparently some of his neighbors heard screams coming from his townhouse, someone even recalled the word "murder" shouted out, but they didn't call the police because they didn't want to intervene, or they didn't know what to do, or they were afraid. Some were likely afraid of the police. I thought about the *Stabroek News*, the Guyanese paper whose articles populate my Twitter feed, and how robberies, stabbings, attacks in Georgetown are daily affairs, and it's shocking for such a small city to be so violent, and I know that Georgetown isn't Kingston, Guyana isn't Jamaica, but what do I know? What do I know about desperation beyond what I read? If people are desperate enough they can find their way through the high gates and the razorwire spiraling atop. And if someone is prepared to invade a home, what else are they capable of? Suddenly the world appears terrifying, predatory, unfair, but West Vancouver insulates me from these realities, so much so that I don't know how to consider them, I don't realize that I, the benefactor of global inequalities, may be the predator.

Until the motivation for Delroy's murder becomes known, it could be any of these things, but I can't ignore that Delroy was gay and visible, beautiful, beloved. In part, that was why I cried. The other source of my tears was one that the news of Delroy's murder reached, a source I'd dammed up for years.

In my undergraduate years in Montréal I studied media, and co-hosted a show on college radio. We covered rallies, concerts, municipal elections, church scandals. We followed stories about police profiling, and discrimination in hiring and housing, but one of the major issues we covered arose in 1998, at the launch of an audio anthology of oral poetry by Black poets from Toronto, Montréal, and Ottawa. The event was covered in all of the local arts weeklies. It was on CBC Radio. Posters were pasted all over downtown. The posters featured a group photo in which a circle of poets beamed upward at the camera.

The event was a success even before the launch. I was jealous. I wanted to be part of that group, but I didn't have any talent for assembling words or for public performance. I could speak on the radio without getting too anxious, but the moment I had to say something in public my face flushed as if I'd been drinking, and my words stammered out. This only increased the nerves, the flush, the stammer. I couldn't imagine standing on a stage in front of a microphone and declaiming a dub poem about the ills of society, maintaining a rhythm and gesturing to punctuate the work, everyone looking up at me as my voice boomed from the speakers.

I participated by interviewing some of the poets. I was moved by their commitment to the idea that language was a transforming agent that, once expressed, acted on the world. They were naïve, young, and I was equally so, and their conviction vibrated inside me. I interviewed a poet named Camilo, who arrived with a group of four of his brethren. They stood behind him in the studio, all of them smelling like nag champa, frankincense, patchouli, freshly rolled marijuana, that sweet skunky smell that permeates hair and clothes. They stroked their chins as they leaned against the studio wall, nodded their heads to the roots music we spun before the interview. After the interview Camilo remained in the studio to listen to the program and chat with me, while his brethren caught night buses uptown to St-Michel.

We discussed musical selections on air and agreed on a dub record from 1981, *Scientist: Your Teeth in My Neck*. I told him I thought it odd that a poet would want to hear music without words, and he said that he loved dub because it taught him so much about how to use words. It was a music of either subtractive or additive syncopation, as he put it. There were only so many instrumental parts. The bass, which was lead, was the one in which both melody and rhythm met. It suggested possible harmonies by emphasizing the fundamental note of any scale, it offered riddims for the horns to punctuate, and it told the organ player where to find the pocket for their bubble. I didn't understand everything he was talking about, but I've thought about it since, and he's correct. There are only so many instrumental parts, so as the dubmaster echoes out and subtracts the horns, then the keyboards, then warbles the vocals out, all that remains may be bass, drums, percussion, and guitar, and if the bass drops out, then only the drums, guitar, and percussion remain, and the dubmaster might start reintroducing the other parts at low volumes, fading them up, until two-thirds of the band is heard together again. The entire sound might be drenched in tape delay, until we don't know which sounds will re-emerge, or how the rhythm will skank and bounce forth, and the music's skank and bounce is enveloped by the hiss of the tape as it rides the reels.

We joked that he, a born Haitian, and I, a child of Guyanese immigrants, should know so much about Jamaican culture. That small island's culture, particularly as it related to music, was dominant throughout the Caribbean and recognized around the world, and we talked about this as we walked out of the station and through the Plateau neighborhood. We walked all the way from University Street, which borders McGill, to St-Laurent Boulevard.

It was October, the leaves were changing, but it was still warm enough to wander outside. St-Laurent had a seedy charm, which it still has, but back then it was more derelict and yet overflowing with students in lines to go to Tokyo, Blizzarts, and other bars. People drank beer out of brown bagged bottles as they walked the street, and where St-Laurent intersected with Prince Arthur, the cobblestones were packed with young people, some lined up to get into Café Campus, some walking to and from St-Louis Square, the park that extends toward St-Denis

Street, and in whose center stands a tall fountain. People were sitting around the fountain smoking joints, strumming guitars.

Water slowly cascaded down into a pool at the base of the fountain. We rolled a spliff. As we smoked, the night reeled backward and forward, trembled, and hissed along slowly. The stars fizzled, and when I asked Camilo how he, a Haitian, acquired a Spanish name, he told me that his parents were Marxists and they named him after the Cuban revolutionary Camilo Cienfuegos.

He told me about Cienfuegos, how beautiful the man was, how he looked like a Cuban military bohemian, and we laughed at that. Cienfuegos always wore fatigues and a cowboy hat over his wild hair. He had an African's curly beard, Camilo thought, and wondered where the Africans were in his lineage. He also noted that after the Haitian Revolution, in the lean years following the retreat of the French, many Haitians fled to Cuba, seeking more favorable conditions. Camilo's theory was that it was those Haitian migrants who delivered the Cubans their revolutionary consciousness. We laughed about that too, and smoked, and stared up past the fountain at the stars.

The night air was cool. We left the park and walked up St-Denis, where Camilo said he had to catch a bus. I waited with him, shivering a bit, and when we saw the bus passing Sherbrooke Street, he took my hand and pulled me to him, then he kissed me. He kissed me on the lips, and then he kissed me again, and then he let me go. I stood back and he mounted the steps of the lighted bus. I watched the bus thread its bulk into the grid of traffic lights and car silhouettes that snaked up St-Denis Street, then I turned and walked home.

I thought about Camilo the week leading up to the show. I didn't know whether I should go. Camilo would likely be tepid with me, and I would have to be the same. I didn't want him to think I was pressuring, and I worried, but I went. A stage stood in one corner of the gallery's ground floor, a bar in another. A mezzanine and a second bar overlooked the main floor. The mezzanine and the main seating area were full. Heads turned and glances crossed. That self-awareness was infectious. I found myself studying the room, noticing that under heavy fall coats and scarves, some people wore dashikis.

I went alone because I wanted to show Camilo that I was still available, but I worried of seeing him with his brethren. I might make him nervous, or embarrass him. I fidgeted without anyone to talk to, and cursed myself for going to the show. I felt stupid and eyed the door, but every time it opened a new hairstyle bobbed through: dreadlocks with sheen, cornrows that bloomed into afro-tufts, blowouts, clean fades. I drifted through the venue, then found a place to stand on the main floor just behind the seating area, next to a concrete pillar. I had a clear view of the stage. In the front row I noticed a table of women, some with shaved heads. I recognized one of them, wearing a checkered newsboy cap, nodding to the music. She was a known house DJ. I scanned the stage, and then admitted to myself that if I saw Camilo I might play him off. I hung back by the pillar sipping a stout, and eventually the lights dimmed and the poets were introduced. One after the other, they took the stage and recited.

The poets were introduced by a young man who wore a sparkling vest with a bowtie, and had his dreadlocks pulled into pigtails. His hair was thick and lush, and he spoke fast, with a slight British-sounding lilt. I couldn't place his accent, but someone later told me that he was Nigerian. One of the male poets strode on stage in an African robe, with a carved walking stick and large wooden beads around his neck, as if mimicking the stereotypical image of the village elder. He emphasized the rhythm of his words by lifting the stick and bringing it down close to the floor.

Most of the poets were young men with assertive deliveries, a cadence punctuated by hand gestures: pointing, slicing, or chopping, sometimes pressing a hand over the heart or pounding the chest, sometimes pointing upward and acknowledging the mezzanine, which prompted a cascade of cheers. The audience responded, drawing gasps as clever phrases turned, crying out when a trenchant observation was made, cheering when the rhetorical sheet was flung off a social bias. A woman from Toronto delivered an energetic narrative poem, in patois, about a character who sold sex to escape from poverty. I remember her exact inflection, where she cut a word short, paused, and where her voice rose in pitch.

The first half of the show ended, the lights and music faded up, and people bought drinks. The mood was jubilant, but there seemed to be some odd tension up front, between the table of women and members of Camilo's crew. It appeared that words were exchanged, voices raised, and a few people bumped up. Tension rippled, then eased. I couldn't tell what had happened. Camilo's friends had their jackets on, big puffy black jackets with furry hoods, and they eventually withdrew and went outside.

At the bar I ran into Bussa, a Bajan trumpet player and poet whom I knew from the radio station. We leaned up together as the show resumed. Camilo's crew came back inside. They stood by the stage with their jackets and hoods on. An odor of smoked weed drifted into the room.

The first poet to be introduced was Camilo, and he stepped onto the stage in dark green cargo pants, suede Wallabees, and a dashiki. He wore his dreadlocks unbound, dangling down to his shoulders, and he hadn't shaved all week. A dark goatee outlined his mouth. Without his winter jacket he looked much skinnier, almost delicate. He fumbled with the height of the microphone, then he fiddled with its angle. He wrung his hands as he introduced his poem. His fingers were slim. I don't remember what he said, but the title of the poem was, "In the Valley of the Damned."

He started into the poem and then stumbled. He stopped. The room was silent. I looked up, and the air seemed suspended in anticipation of his words. The people on the mezzanine stared down to the stage and waited. Smoke floated. Camilo started again, and this time his words issued more naturally, although I detected a slight quaver in his voice. Suddenly his voice found its depth and its range. A stream of words boomed out from the stage monitors. One of his hands raised up and opened as if he were testifying, his mouth twisted and bitterly ejected: "Sodomites," and in slow drawn-out speech, he predicted how, in the valley of the damned, they would reproduce. In an equally acid tone he issued the word "transvestites," and as the word bit into the room, I saw a flutter of movement from the table in the front.

The DJ with the newsboy cap was standing and gesturing toward the stage. Others were on their feet, shouting. One of the women, dressed in a conservative cream-colored waistcoat with a peach scarf and a long weave that reflected the lights, was up on stage pointing at Camilo, advancing toward him while shouting. Camilo looked from her to the audience, and hesitated in his delivery. He stood there, suspended between his poem and silence, glancing at the woman then at the audience. Another woman whom I recognized as a poet was suddenly on the stage, and she snatched the microphone from Camilo's slim hand. In a dry, crackling patois that burst like electricity from the black speakers she dubbed:

HOW

HOW

HOW

HOW

HOW *can yu have a revalueshan*
    without the gay man?

HOW

HOW *can yu have a revalueshan*
widout the lesbian?

She bounced across the stage, her fatigues baggy and her brown leather jacket creaking. She stared down the audience as she spoke, stared them clear in their faces as if daring them to get up on the stage and take the mic by force.

The stage was swarmed by a group of men, mostly poets. There was commotion, hands raised, someone else had the microphone, then someone else, and finally a heavyset Brown man with glasses, a tidy fade, a rasping voice and a sidling, conspiratorial manner was urging people to be calm, to sit back down and feel love, love, it's all love, it's all about love, and give the poet the chance to finish his poem. The women at the table in front were yelling. I was yelling, as was Bussa next to me, as were others, telling him to let the woman finish.

The women who had been seated up front flung up hands and exited the venue amid jostles and jeers. I later heard that several men followed them all the way to the metro. A meanness settled over the celebration, muted the enthusiasm surrounding the release of the CD, at the unity it represented between Caribbean communities in three cities, the initiative of the young people who cleaved together—I could romanticize it, but why?

Instead of giving in to the poetic urge, and to the nostalgia that distorts perspective on our youth, I aim to be critical. What we experienced was a rare moment of collective coming-of-age. It was the moment at which all of those young poets, who had up to that point been performing their identities as artists, and in their per-formance were supported by the audience, became the ideas they espoused. Everyone in the room—even if they didn't understand it—was a witness to it. When that young poet in fatigues, whose name I later found out was d'bi, snatched the microphone, she also stole the emphasis of the evening. She told us that we didn't have to be complacent. We didn't have to live according to our parents' island strictures. It was one of the most courageous things I'd ever seen, although the community media didn't see it that way. The articles emerged questioning her intervention, saying that she violated Camilo's right to free speech. Other community papers praised Camilo's work, and the controversy amid the poets from the three cities surged, but their unity was splintered. Those of us who attended the event, we splintered as well.

I found myself getting my coat from the coatcheck, where I saw Camilo, backed by his crew, arguing with two women. I thought to intervene, but as he was in the middle of some emphatic declaration, he glanced at me out of the corner of his eye and then glanced away. I left. In the week since I'd first met Camilo, the temperature had dropped and autumn had become winter. The cold air itself contained a hint of desolation, a reminder that the Montréal of 1999 was still a post-referendum concrete shell with broken streets, abandoned businesses, and red À LOUER signs in windows. Even down by the Old Port, along St-Antoine street where the *Gazette* churned out newspapers overnight, store windows were boarded and some of the street lamps were out. Trash overflowed from battered *Ville de Montréal* bins. As I walked to the metro I felt lonely and derelict, like the city itself.

It was February. I was at the radio station interviewing a group of women who had established a queer Caribbean womens' social group. They wanted to remain anonymous on air, and they operated with an anonymous email address as their contact. At one point we suspended discussion to play some music, and the phone rang. I answered, and a man's voice, with what sounded like a Trinidadian accent, demanded why I was airing "this gay nonsense." He told me that this was the last time he tuned in to the show. Seconds later the phone rang again, and as I answered I heard a man's voice growling like a dog.

The phone rang a third time. When I answered there was a pause, and then a soft voice sobbed: "How could you do this to me? How could you do this? You bitch. I'm waiting outside the station. When your show finishes I'm going to kick your ass." The man hung up. I went to the window, which overlooked an empty parking lot. I went to the front door of the station, which gave onto a quiet snowy street. When I got back to the on-air studio I told my guests about the calls. We played another song and decided to call some friends to meet us at the station. The phone rang again, and again it was the same voice, now trembling: "How could you? I told you... I'm going to come to the station and kill you—"

"Who is this?"

"..."

"Who is this?"

The voice sobbed, then hissed, "Camilo."

"Fuck you." I said the first thing that came to mind, then hung up the phone. It didn't ring again.

Camilo Cienfuegos disappeared in October 1959 on a night flight in his Cessna. He might have been flying over Florida. Nobody ever found him, and that mystery has enhanced his legend. He is a folk hero, a hero of the revolution. It helps that he looked the part, with his hair so perfectly disheveled it seemed to indicate a readiness for action, his fatigues and his beard worn as a rebuke to people like me and the bourgeois comforts that emphasize my value as a human being. I wouldn't fly in a Cessna under any conditions. As a father I can't be so frivolous. I doubt that I would be able to strap on a rifle and camp in the mountains while preparing a revolutionary overthrow of the government. That seems outrageous to me, like the premise of a video game. I cultivate normalcy. I'm a father and husband. The loudest color I wear is navy. I stay ahead on all my payments, drive a charcoal Volvo sedan to work, studiously avoid debt, and blend in as best I can.

I look up from my Twitter feed and out the window at the tree-lined back lane. The West Vancouver sunlight filters through the leaves. Some days I look out this window and see my daughter playing with her friends while my wife sits at the table on our rear terrace, under the willow tree, reading, then glancing up from her Paule Marshall novel, and something about this is so idyllic, so radiant when compared to the brick and broken streets, the sullen darkness and cold of Montréal, that I wish time would stop and this moment would extend forever in both directions, into the past so it erases everything and is all that I remember, and into the future so it's all we ever experience, this muted, unassuming joy.

I don't know what happened to Camilo. When I was still in Montréal I used to run into one of his friends, Marron, who wore long dreadlocks and always sported a black flak jacket. A few years after the incident he cut his locks and returned to school. His style gradually adapted from denim to khaki slacks, hoodies to navy blazers, sneakers to oxfords. He lost touch with Camilo. He told me that Camilo suffered thyroid problems and gained weight. He wasn't writing anymore. He was living with his parents in the suburbs, in Rivière-des-Prairies, and working as an orderly at a hospital. He experienced a burst of notoriety in the community after the incident, and was invited to recite his poems on radio programs, at hip hop showcases, on panels. But after that initial notoriety faded, the invitations slowed and Camilo slid into depression.

Marron told me that they all tried to rally Camilo for a while. They would visit him at his parents' house and drop off CDs, books, vegetarian rotis from his favorite shop, the rotis with the pumpkin in them, or pakoras, which he loved. Sometimes Camilo would emerge and hang out, but he would be subdued, distant, and would eventually withdraw to his room. After a while he stopped emerging for anything other than meals and work. In my last year in Montréal I no longer ran into Marron, or any of the other poets from my college radio days. My job took me to Vancouver, and I was happy to leave the dingy brick city.

On my way to the airport I sat back in the taxi as we drove over the Turcot expressway, with its crumbling concrete and exposed iron wires. The flat gravel rooftops of

St-Henri flashed past below, and clotheslines floated in the breeze. I could see small specks of teenagers playing on the basketball courts, and the green copper roofs above the stone churches, and I was seized with a feeling of anger toward the Caribbean community, its smallness, its self-consciousness, and its insularity. That anger resurges even today. When it does, I feel righteous for wanting my children to grow up as far from that community as possible, and when it recedes I despise myself for my weakness. But most days I don't think about any of this at all. I drink my espresso, I calculate the fastest way to pay off my mortgage, I worry about my children, I arrive early to work. I live.

Navette

SOMEWHERE IN THIS STORY is a break, a portal, a black hole. It may only be the size of a small pothole on Crémazie Boulevard, or the size of a period between sentences, a semicolon, a semicolony, a sixteenth note's round head, or an island that looks like ink spilled onto the blue map. In 1972 a young woman fell through such an inkspill, one called *Ayiti,* and a young man reached for her hand and was pulled in after her. They were my grandparents.

As they tumbled, they pulled their children in with them. They planned to land somewhere, but couldn't guess that their imagined somewhere was just another cypher to plunge through. They tumbled with their bank accounts up in the air, the furniture on which they were still making payments hovering, their credit score falling into their job at the factory, their son's university education falling into his uncle's yellow taxi, and the inflections of their *Kreyòl* climbing the air alongside the black faces that don't crack as they plummet past 40, as the mercury blindly plunges in January with the hopes of the entire displaced tropical community whose brick brownstones tumble in zero gravity, whose paychecks flutter, whose voices spiral toward the stars while thuggish cops somersault over the moon and land nowhere as their truncheons fly past heads and their bullets zip along the brims of baseball caps, as the scent of *diri kolé ak pwa* insulates against the winter that snows down atop everyone.

My parents showed little interest in travel, even though it was an interest they could afford. They migrated with their parents in the early days of Baby Doc Duvalier's régime, when he was the only adolescent in the world to bear the title *président à vie*. Even with that outlandish title and the millions he would steal, he would still fall. Just like so many of his countrymen and women, he would lead a fugitive existence, although those compatriots, like my parents, lacked the cushion of luxury.

In the early 1800s, in the lean years after the Haitian Revolution, some members of my family fled to Cuba. It is rumored that they sailed on a makeshift raft, crooked branches lashed together with vine, and that some were lost, but rumor is often repeated until it binds itself to memory, and once bound, is launched into history. What happened on arrival? I imagine their *Kreyòl* was hammered by work, sun, and circumstance into Spanish, and that they darkened into the Cuban population. How many generations did it take before they learned to roll an R with the tip of the tongue? Maybe their descendants passed their revolutionary worldview on to the Cubans. None of this can be confirmed. What I do know is that the crossing on a raft was an echo of an earlier, equally harrowing passage.

In grade school my friends' parents planned summer trips to Hawai'i. When I asked my parents if we could go, my father kissed his teeth and tossed up his hand. "Your whole family is here, in Montréal. Why would we go sleep on a volcano?" My mother quoted an afterschool special. "If you want to travel, then pick up a book." *The Hitchhiker's Guide to the Galaxy* became my companion. I wasn't interested in science fiction so I didn't read it, but I fell in love with the title.

My mother always stressed that a person must have "purpose and direction." She never specified further, and I never asked, but she pronounced "direction" with conviction, as if it were an exact location. I often wondered whether direction was internal and conceptual, and only sometimes mapped itself onto the physical world, and even when it did, it remained endless, and thereby distinct from destination. My father used to tell me that the fastest way to get from one place to the next was to travel in a straight line, not a zigzag or a circle or a revolution. The lesson learned from Haiti and Cuba and Québec's *Révolution tranquille* was that *la révolution ne mène nulle part.*

Montréal North orbited the city, a satellite made of concrete and brick. Our language—*Kreyòl*—sustained its sonic orbit of French. All of us in Montréal North were suspended between here and elsewhere, between a temporary home and nowhere, between uncertainties, urgencies, between the Vietnamese *épicier* and the Québécois landlord, always with a fugitive spirit abiding, a flight instinct dormant but alive in case things turned nasty, as they did after a drunken Jacques Parizeau blamed 1995's failed referendum on *l'argent et le vote ethnique.*

Je me souviens. That was the only time my parents ever talked about going anywhere. They whispered the words *Towontó* and *'Amiltón* for months. Evenings my father and grandfather held hushed discussions over maps, calculators, U-Haul pamphlets, and crooked columns of numbers inked on the backs of Hydro-Québec envelopes. Listening from the next room, pretending to do my homework, which consisted of identifying the planets and moons of our solar system, I felt myself lifted out of my familiar Montréal. I asked my mother what *Towontó* was like, and whether people spoke French there, and she laughed and quipped that Toronto was in a different country. Toronto might well have been a different galaxy. The U-Haul never materialized.

At 15 I ran away from home. It was November, the time of year when days darken at 4 pm and windows frost over. I left early. My parents were still asleep, but my grandparents were awake, talking softly in their room. I hurried past row houses, shoeboxes, apartment complexes topped by billboards, all different shades of brick, and then the veined concrete structure of the *métropolitaine* rose up. I hesitated among the semi-vacant office buildings with broken windows, feeling the cold settle over me. The concrete vibrated and amplified the car engines, and I worried that someone would recognize me. I glanced back toward the apartment blocks huddled together, then raised my arm and stuck out my thumb.

The driver was a chubby, chatty man with long hair tied back in a ponytail. Once we turned onto the expressway he asked, *tu connais-tu Mary-Jane?* And then he laughed. I told him I didn't know her. He seemed to think he knew something I didn't and he insisted, but are you sure you don't know Mary-Jane? You're young and you're hitchhiking and you don't know Mary-Jane? That's very strange. He gave me a funny look and chuckled again. I told him again that I didn't know her. He went silent. Where the cityscape tapered into long low industrial buildings, he dropped me off.

I walked backward along the shoulder and managed to hitch another ride with an off-duty cabbie in a brown suit. He said he was going my way, and didn't say anything else. We listened to Haitian radio, the host in conversation with people back home. He let me off by a roadside diner where I lingered over eggs and sausages, surreptitiously glancing over the rim of my coffee at the truckers and farmers whose French twanged.

A few kilometers outside of Lennoxville, a silver Econoline shot past me. Along its side the word "shuttle" was spray painted in ornate cursive. The letters raced against a cosmic backdrop. The van swung to the shoulder and I jogged to meet it. A dreadlocked man with dark brown skin leaned out of the side door: "Boo. Get in." I got in. Four people were in the van, one black and three white. The van swung back onto the road, and one of the passengers lit a spliff. Its smoke curled amid a tangle of electric jazz. One of the white passengers, with a beard in tufts and his hair tied up in a top-knot, passed me the spliff and exhaled: "Headhunters," as he nodded to the music. I smoked, just to be polite. It was dusk when I got out in Lennoxville. The shuttle swerved back onto the highway and I watched it flash into the distance and disappear.

Time seemed to have slowed. I could feel heat and smoke wafting off me, and the night soaring above. I wandered in and out of a few shops. The clerks eyed me, and in a clothing store one followed me from afar, hid behind a mannequin and peeked over its bare white shoulder. I gave up my browsing. I found an empty café and ordered a soup and sandwich. I wandered over to a tall bookshelf. Written along the first spine that I saw, right at eye-level, were the words: *The Hitchhiker's Guide to the Galaxy*.

The clerk brought me my soup and sandwich and told me the café would be closing soon. I got scared and asked if I could borrow the phone. I called my parents. My father shouted at me, told me I deserved "licks like fire," and that "sparks" would "fly" off me when he got hold of me. He then spoke calmly to the owner and convinced him to let me stay in the café for another two hours, while he drove out from the city.

At 18 I was accepted to the Université du Québec à Montréal. I moved into the city. It was the first time I experienced the upheaval of boxes and the stress of gathering needed things. It was the first time I lived anywhere other than the home into which I had been born. My parents were mystified: *Mais pourquoi veux-tu aller vivre dans un quartier louche alors que tu peux rester ici chez nous? Ici on s'occupe de tout. On exige seulement que tu réussisses tes études. Tu n'as même pas à travailler ni à payer de loyer.* Why would I want to go live in a little apartment in some jumbled neighborhood when I could stay in my parents' house? All I had to do was succeed, and they would take care of everything else. According to their genetic compass, my moving out was a step backward. I couldn't argue with their genetic compass, but mine was equally magnetic, and it drew me toward a move. It pointed me away from the old neighborhood and deeper into the city. The only explanation I could offer was that I wanted *mon indépendance*. My father scoffed, *indépendance de qui?* From whom? From us? We who work to pay for this house and this food? So you interpret our painstaking support as subjection? And when my mother realized that my conviction was as firm as the crumbling city infrastructure, she drily commented, *vive le jeune Québécois libre*.

One of my mother's mantras was that each generation needs to do better than the previous. She never explained "do better," and I was too afraid to vex her with my naïveté, so I never asked what it meant. Did it mean that I had to migrate to even more far-flung metropoles, establish myself where nobody in my family had ever been? Did I have to amass more money, acquire a more valued position in some profession, or simply do things that nobody else who shared my bloodline had ever done? For instance, if there had never been an itinerant rum-drinking visionary in my family, did that mean that the option was open to me? Did this mean that my rum-fired cosmic visions ought to be my destination? Did it mean that I had to be happier than my parents, who were supposed to be happier than their parents? The message was conflicted, because in order to "do better" I had to step out of their orbit, and while they must have known this, they gave no indication. I never asked whether the idea of generational advancement was sustainable. At some point, wouldn't there be a limit on the success we could achieve? Wasn't success a kind of consumption?

My Uncle Maximilien is stardust now, shimmering somewhere along a gust of solar wind, but on January 28, 1986, the *Challenger* space shuttle exploded just after lift-off, and on February 6, the Duvalier régime was overthrown, and my uncle was moved to mysticism. He founded his own non-denominational church. That church is stardust now. To him, these events revealed that the human being is unable to go as far as she wants because she is bound by the body, but the spirit can travel, the spirit is everywhere at once. He believed that the spirit is here in Montréal while simultaneously being in *Ayiti* and in Africa, alive in all times past, present, and future, and that people need to be awakened to the fact, and once awakened, to make cosmic leaps in time and space. He preached a spiritual return to Africa, his mantra: "Prayer is my shuttle."

I took a part-time job driving a taxi on evenings and weekends. It was an embarrassment. According to my father, *un pas en arrière*. A step backward. My parents were professionals who felt they had earned the right to consider themselves a class apart from the taxi drivers, *buanderie* operators, and *dépanneur* owners. They couldn't imagine me arguing at the taxi stand with men from Gonaïves and Port-au-Prince, in their pork-pie hats and bright gold bracelets. *Pourquoi pas Starbuck?* Even *le télémarketing* was preferable. They cringed at the idea of a family friend hailing my cab and recognizing me. I cringed too, always worried that the next fare would be a church acquaintance, but

Montréal's narrow, pocked streets are more populous than they appear, and I enjoyed the role of anonymous driver. I could be invisible behind the steering wheel. I found a freedom in always being on the move, and a satisfaction in reaching a destination quickly and then taking off toward another. I was part of the dashboard's incandescent numbers and dials, by whose light I learned all of the city's major potholes, shortcuts, *ruelles,* and *détours.*

I spent hours queued at the airport, listening to the jet engines crescendo and then fade up into the blue. I would imagine I was in one of the planes going to Dakar, Abidjan, or Kinshasa. Then a big international flight would land and everyone would file outside for a cab. After three hours of sitting reclined in the driver's seat, sweating in the July sun, reading the community papers over again, listening to the CBC's neutrally accented voices discuss incremental declines in the interest rate, or the state of global terror, my cab smelling of sweat, asphalt, and faux leather, I'd get a fare. *Stade Olympique. 2270 rue Hochelaga entre Fullum et Parthenais, Centre Bell, Vieux-port, rue Sherbrooke coin St-Denis, Station Centrale, Maisonneuve coin Peel, Beaubien coin Chambord, Kirkland, Rive-sud, Villeneuve et Jeanne-Mance*, it didn't matter.

I opened the door for a woman with a saxophone. Her head was half-shaved, half sprouting long dreadlocks, some graying. She carried her saxophone case into the back seat. White stenciled lettering along one side of the case read: **ROCKET NUMBER 9**. I asked her where she wanted to go and she said: just head downtown. I asked if there was a particular location or address, and she instructed me to drop her in the middle of the city. She would find her way. We detoured around construction sites and around excavated stretches of road, and finally reached the massive, crumbling Turcot interchange. I drove her into the Old Port, and dropped her off near the Maisonneuve monument, with the green Iroquois figure squatting at its base and looking into the distance. I wheeled into a line of taxis and took my place. She walked up to the monument, then reached out and touched the forehead of the squatting figure. She opened Rocket Number 9 on the cobblestones and started playing.

My grades slipped. I couldn't bear to immerse myself in theories of inflation, explanations of supply and demand, while waiting for fares. Macroeconomics was tedious when compared to navigating the Plateau streets at night. I sat in my cab and left the radio tuner between stations, where the static was most dense. The hiss and roar surged, as if my cab were adrift on the Atlantic. I watched people pour out of Mont-Royal metro, and other people pour in. Sometimes I stood outside my cab and smoked. I listened to the older men argue about the leadership vacuum in *Ayiti*. I always wondered why they spoke about home so much after having spent decades in Montréal. I had never been to Haiti, so I guessed that Haiti was a country that had seen everything, and where one could see everything, all of the conditions of existence played out in the streets. Montréal was not like that. Even when the students were on strike, and thousands were marching and beating pots and pans in an act of mass public defiance, it was a well-fed defiance. Most of the protestors would return home to find food in the fridge, so there was something playful about that defiance, something of an uptown summer *fête*.

As the strike continued, a deep restlessness pulled at me. Some nights when I didn't have a fare I would drive through the Plateau, wasting the gas I'd bought. I'd smoke a spliff and concentrate on the pattern I was driving—for instance a large square figure eight that stretched from St-Denis to Papineau, or a triangle, which was my favorite, and which stretched from Pie-ix to Greene, and then up to Van Horne. Sometimes I'd drive through Villeray and park in an open lot just in front of the Crémazie elevated expressway, roll down the windows, and listen to the vibration of cars amplified by the concrete, the swish and hum populating the night, multiplying with the traffic and gradually dying, only to multiply again. Sometimes I ignored possible fares and just sat listening. Sometimes the hum became such a deep rumble that the concrete expressway itself sounded like a massive engine, a rocket booster, the whole structure vibrating as if about to propel the city upward.

My parents worried that I would turn out like my uncle Maximilien. His cosmic mysticism and the strange conclusions he drew from observing world events forced my parents and my grandparents to question his equilibrium. Each decision I made—to move out, to moonlight as a taxi driver, to question whether I should take time off school or go right back into my second year, to support the student strike with my vote and by attending demonstrations—struck my parents as contrary, and their incomprehension made me question myself.

1986: The news from home announced sustained protests, violence, and uncertainty, yet Baby Doc Duvalier declared his regime "as firm as a monkey's tail." People fled the island. Haitians in Montréal North and St-Michel worried about extra rooms and extra bellies to fill, of further dividing apartments to accommodate one or two relatives, if necessary.

On January 28, 1986, the space shuttle *Challenger* was scheduled to take off. My uncle was fixated on the sole African-American crew member, Ronald Erwin McNair. Ronald McNair played the saxophone, and he planned to take his saxophone on board and record a solo while in space. My uncle was very serious about what this symbolized. For him, the outer space conceit that existed in some Black music, the shiny metallic costumes, the lunar landscapes on album covers, the shuttle cockpits whose consoles were synthesizers, Sun Ra's belief that he was born on another planet, and the general idea that music was a kind of ephemeral space vessel, would be revealed as both vanity and prophecy. Vanity because here was a man who was not getting high, who was not pretending to be a cosmic traveler while playing a synthesizer, but who was in fact an astronaut, and who was going to make music in outer space. On the other hand, what if all of the costumes, antics, and fantasies of interstellar travel prefigured this moment. The launch of the *Challenger*, with Ronald McNair and his saxophone on board, sent the message that Black music would be at the forefront of the future, leading people beyond the inanities and indignities of police profiling, second class citizenry, Reaganomics, referendums, dictatorships, fear, and flight.

Ronald McNair's *Challenger* flight was not about fleeing. It was about purpose and direction. The *Challenger* lifted off, but it exploded seconds after it broke the sound barrier.

On February 7, 1986, the Duvalier regime was toppled, and Baby Doc himself was on a plane to France, fleeing for his safety.

The dominant myth in my family, and sometimes it seems in my community, is that each generation must do better, must exceed the successes of the previous. My uncle believed that this wasn't possible. Depressions, earthquakes, dictatorships, could hinder any generation's progress, and given such hindrances, each generation would have to re-evaluate the meaning of progress for themselves. Perhaps, in the case of my grandparents, progress simply meant getting out of *Ayiti* with their families intact, and re-establishing life in a quiet working class suburb of Montréal, visiting the flea market on the weekends with their grandchildren, and listening to the news from home on shortwave radio.

For the media, progress was a graduation from the torpor of the Antilles to the opportunity and sobriety of Canada. For my father, progress meant becoming an accountant, and for my mother becoming a teacher, working and saving money, and staying close to family. For my uncle, the picture was much more confused. A person who did what was expected, who followed the "straight and narrow," might still get divorced, might still be dismembered in an automobile accident, might still be crushed by a dictator, or stricken with illness. Progressing blindly wasn't any solution to the arbitrariness and violence of life, to the fact that there are no rules and that there is no direction. A person who obtains a master's degree might become an alcoholic and lose their job, might become despised by their children. An orphan from Cap-Haïtien might become the super middleweight world boxing champion, wearing Armani suits and custom made jewelry, a hero to every boy in St-Michel.

A middle-aged French couple hailed my cab at the intersection of de Maisonneuve and Crescent, right in the downtown party district. Their faces were flushed and they talked loudly. The woman directed: *Chambord et St-Zotique, sur Visa*, and then embraced her companion. Downtown, several police blockades were in place, and we had to drive much farther east before we were able to start going north. Down by the Quartier des Spectacles, the streets were blocked off for a festival. Crowds streamed along the sidewalks and trickled between the cars stopped at lights. The couple seemed oblivious to everything but themselves. Their eyes were closed as they ran hands over each other.

I turned south. A group of students broke into a run, and behind them a line of *flics* in riot gear advanced, rhythmically beating their shields with truncheons. Two cops ran up to the car, banged on the hood, pointed and shouted for me to drive back up the street down which I had just come. I turned around in my seat and reversed, with the couple in the back blind to everything outside their embrace. I then came to a street that was taped off, with cops at each corner.

I had the dial tuned to Haitian radio, and it was playing an old soukouss song by Tabu Ley Rochereau: *En amour y a pas de calcul*, which loosely translates as: there is no formula for love. My grandparents had never been able to resist the old Congolese love songs. If one of their favorites came on the radio, they would even truncate a discussion of where their lives would have been had they remained in Haiti, to listen. I inherited their love for the Congolese rhumba, for soukouss, for that song in particular.

My windows were open and the damp air drifted through my cab. The kickdrum was sustaining a forceful four-on-the-floor. The shuttle-shaped tips of the drumsticks were speeding a 16th-note pattern along the rim of the hi-hat. The hi-hat ticked itself between each drumbeat. Occasionally the drummer would stagger his beat with a fill on the snare, or a low bomb on the floor tom. I felt the rhythm in my spine and hips. I could feel it in my knees and I could feel each hi-hat lick spark along my teeth. Two rhythm guitars were plucking different patterns, each playing against waves of soft distortion from their old tube amplifiers and from the dust collected on the magnetic tape in the studio, the dust pressed into the vinyl, each guitar splintering reverberant notes among the undulations of the conga counter-rhythms. The music was like water or fire or air, elemental, as it surged and retreated. It was there and it was nowhere. It was in the speakers but it was also in me and in the night. The lead guitar was stringing together a supple and serpentine riff that repeated, but each time it repeated, one or two notes were added or subtracted, punctuation and void. Where did they go? The horn section was laying out, counting, feeling the music's time, and Tabu Ley hovered in silence and waited for the one to revolve before swinging his high lead voice back into the mix: *Le vrai amour est spontané, sans contrainte. Ne me fais pas trop d'exigences, car je t'aime.* The bassline seemed to move forward and back at the same time. Some of the band members yelled out in the background.

The syncopation struck out geometric patterns in my mind. *Y a pas deux calculs. Y a pas deux mesures.* The drumbeat suddenly became very focused and unforgiving. It shot forward. Two guitars and the bass dropped out. The drums continued, four on the floor, insisting, with the hi-hat ticking stardust around each beat, making each beat shine and glimmer. The voice rose like smoke off the rhythm, like heat off the asphalt, or like an airplane off the runway. *Ou on aime ou on n'aime pas. Ou on aime chaud ou on aime froid.* Police sirens raised themselves out of the darkness and flashed off the windows of buildings. The horn section pushed its melody through brazen air. The traffic stopped. The students ran. A cop blew a whistle and tried to wave a bus through the jam. Tired faces stared out the windows of the lighted bus.

I thought of my uncle, my parents, my grandparents. The entire band swooped back in and the music rose up out of the tinny car radio, up off the floor of the cab, up out of the windows and into the night, scattering radio static among the stars, bouncing it off the planet, breaking time into a billion micro-syncopations. The hi-hat ticked into the sky over Montréal, over the new condominiums and the disorder of everyday striving. I turned up the volume as far as it would go, opened the door and stepped out. The summer air stuck to me. I walked. The cars behind me honked. The couple in the back seat tightened their embrace as Tabu Ley's high voice soared: *Y a pas de calcul. Y a pas de mesure.* The music shuttled into the night.

Capital

IT WAS TWILIGHT IN the permanent collection. Each painting was accompanied by a caption and a date that reached far back into the colonial period. We emerged squinting into the morning light flooding the mezzanine. The light emphasized Angélique's pallor, and in that moment she seemed like a stranger. We had been bickering all morning, and I wondered how much distance had grown between us. We looked down to the main floor, its massive gray tiles, and out the grid of windows that reached to the roof. We stared over the frozen canal, the denuded trees in the winter sun, and I waited for her to disagree with me. The Houses of Parliament rose atop a hill in the distance. Their weathered stone and the patina of their copper roofs seemed permanent, as if the present itself were a colonial painting composed in 1759.

I leaned on the railing next to Angélique. She withdrew her arm, but the tension remained. I thought about *The Death of General Wolfe*, about the triangulated focus of the painting, how it guided the viewer's gaze past Wolfe collapsed like a messiah in the arms of his doctors and generals, and up to the British flag, bunched and fallen, in the arms of a soldier. These two sentimental embraces, of the flag of empire and of its martyr, mirror one another. Somehow, though, the painting succeeds in spite of this extravagance. If we remove all of its ornaments, it narrates the death of a man important to others, and those others are gathered around him in various attitudes of anxiety, dejection, despair. We believe their expressions. The cooler gray heads of the doctor and the senior generals seem to know that Wolfe will die, with bullets that have torn through his red coat and pierced his torso, and they only seem intent on comforting him in his last moments. The others, the wounded soldiers at a loss for direction, steady themselves against their fellows as they look on in anguish and disbelief.

Columns of smoke rise in the distance and darken the corner of the painting that hangs above the dying general. A messenger rushes up, but Wolfe is about to expire, and the messenger is forever frozen in his approach. He never arrives. He bears the message that the French surrendered after only 16 minutes of battle, that General Montcalm was shot in the stomach, and that, in spite of the turmoil, the British Empire will raise its flag over the *Plaines d'Abraham* again.

The most compelling character in the painting is the Indigenous warrior in the foreground, conspicuously kneeling in the pose of Rodin's *Thinker*, staring at General Wolfe. His mouth is open, tucked down at its corners, and his expression is ambiguous. He is clearly moved. By turns he looks concerned, as anyone would be at the violent death of another human being, but there is some confusion in his look. The messenger hasn't yet arrived with his news, and in the frozen imminence of the painting, he never will. Maybe the confusion arises because he doesn't feel anything. Maybe he realizes that, as Gwendolyn Brooks later wrote, "nobody loves a master." He also looks like he's about to speak, to pronounce something, but will he speak to himself, will he address everyone gathered at Wolfe's side, or will he speak straight to the dying general, perhaps offering a prayer to speed Wolfe to the afterlife, or a curse? Or will he suddenly turn to face the person viewing the painting and say, "make sure that this painting stays in the basement of the National Gallery forever, and that all of the Indigenous art is housed on the top floor," and I am the only one who hears this commentary. I then wonder whether he's laughing at the melodrama of the scene, at the romantic colonial ambitions of the painter, at the way in which General Wolfe seems to be swooning like a lover spurned.

And then we were out of the permanent collection. I turned to Angélique and said, "The Indigenous art should not be in the fucking basement, across from the washrooms, while the colonial art is up here on the second floor."

"Oho, this from a musician," Angélique remarked. She then measured her tone, "Suppose we did make that switch, then what would we move to the basement? Would we move the Group of Seven?"

"Yes. Stash them in the basement."

Angélique snickered. "Or the colonial painters like Joseph Légaré and Benjamin West? This is the National Gallery *of Canada*. Its sole purpose is to tell the story of Canada, not to advocate for social justice."

"But some of those colonial painters weren't even Canadian. They were Irish, British, French. And plus, Canada didn't even exist back then, it was just a colony, so we can take some narrative liberties. Their paintings can hang right across from the washrooms."

"This conversation is too obvious."

"Obvious?"

"Just write your Twitter essay and scrap it out there, but not with me."

"Oh so we're fighting now? That's fitting. If that collection shows Canada emerging out of a contest of nations, then we have to admit that the contest—conquest—is ongoing."

"Or not."

"Angélique, what is your point?"

"What is your point? I was just enjoying the exhibit. Sure it has its problems, but do we have to politicize every fucking thing?"

"Everything is politicized. Plus, I grew up in Toronto, where the Group of Seven was lorded over us like the arrival point of all culture, to the exclusion of everyone else. If that isn't political—"

"Sure, okay, okay, okay, fine. You can have your politics, but you know I have to be here for my thesis, so let me have my own thoughts about the exhibit. You don't have to assault and undermine everything."

"You're wrong. I do have to critique and subvert everything, and I will. If you want your thesis to have any teeth, you should too. That's the point."

"Don't make your point in my ear." Angélique turned

back into the exhibit. I stood on the landing and stared toward Parliament. I didn't know how our fragile civility would endure the trip back to Montréal.

Earlier that year I was in Québec City playing a jazz series. After the show we sat around drinking, and one of the musicians, a contrebasse player who grew up in Québec, displayed an unusual laugh. It was the classic laugh of a Marvel villain, a sonorous Mwa-ha-ha-ha-ha that started out in the mid-register, then deepened and resonated as his mouth opened wider and wider. People at other tables glanced over each time he laughed. After several rounds of drinks and an equal number of trips outside to smoke, one of the musicians asked him where the laugh came from.

He let out the loudest laugh of the evening, one that interrupted the conversations at neighboring tables, then he grinned, "I got it on July 11th, 2004."

Someone else asked, "You remember the exact date? How is that possible? A laugh doesn't have a date of birth. Are you serious?"

"Oh yeah, I'm serious. Does anyone remember what happened on July 11th, 2004?"

Nobody offered any ideas. He hinted, "It was on the *Plaines d'Abraham*." We shook our heads.

"It was during the *Festival d'été de Québec*, and it was raining nonstop. The festival headliner was the French punk band *Bérurier noir*, and 50 thousand people showed up for the concert. The entire Plains was churned into mud. People were covered in mud. Apparently, the stage had to be squeegeed before the performance because so much water gathered on it. At one point I swear I saw the stage crackle blue with electricity.

"At the time I played in a band called *Bomb la bourse*, which was an atrocious name, and my ambition was to gig in Montréal." He lifted up his shirt and exposed his skinny brown flank, where the flesh was raised into an A with a circle around it. He grinned as he dropped his shirt.

"I got high and then got separated from my friends at the concert, and there were so many people, it was getting dark, I couldn't find my way back so I just wandered. I got soaked and took in all the people. It was overwhelming, exciting, like—"

He went quiet and glanced down. We watched his face.

"Imagine that on the Plains, every subculture of Québec punk was represented, from the street squeegees to—I didn't know this at the time—several different groups of fachos, who—"

"What's a facho?"

"A fascist, a Nazi. Some of them were up from Montréal. They had been planning for the event for months, and their sole purpose was to disrupt the concert and rumble. I had no idea about this, and I unknowingly wandered into their camp. All I remember is being soaked through, and looking around at the punks, but not really at anyone in particular, just taking in the vastness of the wet, muddy scene. It was incredible, and suddenly a couple of big *Québs* were shoving me around and yelling at me: *Qu'est-ce-tu fais icitte toé? Qu'est-ce-tu fais icitte LeBrun?* They stank like beer. Others were laughing, and some drunk chick said, "Hey just leave 'im alone... *hostie d'*fuckin' skinny Paki, go back where 'e come from," and there was more laughter, then someone was pouring beer over my head, and then there was a massive commotion. Someone else grabbed me, people were shouting, then punches were being thrown, and I was being shoved in some direction, and there was a lot of shouting and surging, as if the Plains themselves tilted and everyone lost their balance, but it wasn't that. It was some antifa from Montréal—"

"What's antifa?"

"Are you kidding? Anti-fascists. Yeah, some big antifa dudes from Hochelaga, Pointe-St-Charles, Verdun, they'd heard about what the fachos were planning and decided to confront them on the Plains, and there I was, a totally stoned, oblivious Brown dude who wandered through the middle of it and set off a White race riot. I don't know what happened after that though, because I got jostled around and then I popped out the other end of the rumble. I was standing by a group of stoned punks who were from Montréal as well, and who offered me a beer and a smoke and said: "You look like you need it, man." So I took the beer, and I shared a joint with them, and—"

The bassist stared into his lap. He looked back up.

"And then I remember feeling like... like... you're gonna think I'm crazy: I felt like I had a trillion ultra-ultra-slim acupuncture needles covering my cranium. The needles felt good, and they reached up into the air, miles and miles above the clouds, and out through the hole in the ozone layer. As the earth rotated, the needles swayed in one direction and then another, tickling my cranium. It felt incredible, like my head was somehow plugged into the cosmos and was receiving electric impulses from some-where beyond the stratosphere.

"And then I kind of came to my senses a couple of days later, standing outside a metro station shouting at a public telephone. I was eventually picked up, and hospitalized, and prescribed medication. My parents brought me home, and ever since then I've had that laugh. The only thing is, I don't know where I went over those two days, how I got from the concert in Québec to downtown Montréal, or anything that happened to me. I've always wondered whether I'll ever remember, whether I want to remember."

He grinned and let out a sonorous laugh, but everyone else stayed quiet.

"When my parents finally took me home, my dad thought I needed healing music, so he played Alice Coltrane records over and over: *Journey In Satchidananda*, *Ptah the El Daoud*, *Universal Consciousness*, *Eternity*, *World Galaxy*. I realized that the music was delivering a message to me alone. Only I could decode it. The message was that I would understand the message only if I devoted my life to music that communicated peaceably with all living things, as an antidote to the rage and consternation of the world."

I turned away from the view of the frozen canal, of Parliament Hill rising in the distance, the age of its buildings comforting yet disturbingly permanent. I felt an ache for my horn, a desire for its sound to emerge as loud as it would from the speakers on the *Plaines d'Abraham*. I wanted to stand on the mezzanine and play—not a melody, but a stream of expletive notes, ones that would crack the stones of Parliament, sunder the foundations from the earth. The buildings would tremble, lean, and in a blurred streak of color, slide into the canal.

Angélique had slipped back into the permanent collection. I knew she was contemplating *The Death of General Wolfe*. She could sit there for as long as she needed. I texted Angélique and told her I would be heading to the train station, where she could meet me when she was ready.

I took the train back to Montréal alone. For the duration of the ride I kept seeing the same image of Angélique sitting in front of the the painting, examining every figure, trying to identify something of herself, something of her world in the immutable drama of that tableau.

Ashes and Juju

EVERY YEAR TOWARD the end of January I think of a film I'd like to direct. I can't decide what its defining genre would be, but it would start with a tightly framed shot of a man who looks like me. The shot would open outward, gradually. He—I—wearing a lightweight gray wool suit, would be on the 9th floor of the Concordia University Hall Building glancing left and right, deciding which way to go. As I decide, color slowly bleeds from the film. The walls, the doors, the linoleum, the thin metal of the lockers become a grainy, faded sepia.

I hear my name shouted. My scalp tingles. I don't know who is shouting, but I know I have to hurry to them. I turn down an endless corridor bordered by lockers. The corridor bends until it seems I've traveled in a circle. I stop. I look back. The corridor continues in both directions.

I look ahead and realize I'm shifting gears in my Opel, hugging the curves on a narrow street near Lausanne. The road squiggles and winds through forest, and the sunlight flashes down between the trees, glazing my windshield for a second before giving way to shadow. The Opel accelerates, and just as I round a corner I see the car I'm

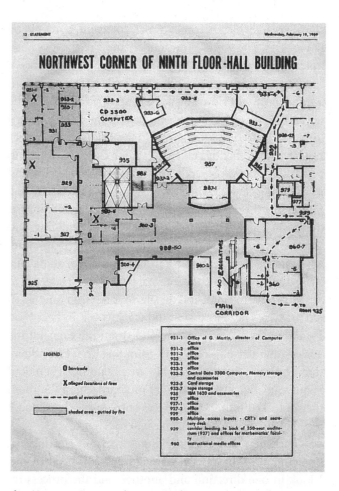

NORTHWEST CORNER OF NINTH FLOOR-HALL BUILDING

LEGEND:

0 barricade

X alleged locations of fires

— — — — path of evacuation

[shaded box] shaded area - gutted by fire

931-1	Office of G. Martin, director of Computer Centre
931-2	office
931-3	office
933	office
933-1	office
933-2	office
933-3	Control Data 3300 Computer, Memory storage and accessories
933-5	Card storage
933-7	tape storage
935	IBM 1620 and accessories
927	office
927-1	office
927-2	office
929	office
980-5	Multiple access inputs - CRT's and secretary desk
939	corridor leading to back of 350-seat auditorium (937) and offices for mathematics' faculty
960	instructional media offices

chasing: a copper Volvo. I accelerate. The amphetamines I swallowed before breakfast sharpen my focus, and as sweat dapples my forehead the road bends again and I lose sight of the Volvo. The trees cast a mottled shadow on the sinewy road, which becomes a corridor again, bordered by tan lockers. The voices grow louder, and I realize I've been holding my breath.

The corridor never reaches the voices. They trail into a thin wail, and I slow down. I can see black smoke at the far end of the corridor, billowing along the ceiling toward me, and I hear a crackling sound that gets louder the farther I go. The air gets hot and the corridor closes in. I have to backtrack. The voices recede, my heart rate accelerates, and its speeding and slowing become the soundtrack to the film, a low thump that resonates through the building. At this point I always wonder whether I am the building, and whether everything in the film is actually happening somewhere inside me. I get lost in a recursive image of a small me struggling to negotiate the internal passages of a larger me.

A fire alarm rings, and the alarm is red iron tongues in red mouths. The voices clang and scream over my heartbeat. I stand in the narrow passage and strain my ears, but the voices—the alarm—seem to be sounding from every direction. I have to cover my ears. They are screaming: "Hamidou! Hamidou!" But just as I think I'm approaching the room they're locked into, as my fingers encircle the doorknob, I recoil in anguish, scorched. I have to backtrack.

Then I'm alone in the quiet corridor. Its lockers, linoleum, and fluorescent lights gleam far ahead of me. I look in one direction and another, and the process re-starts, then grows increasingly harrowing before fading and re-starting again. After a few repetitions I understand the parameters of the adventure, as one understands the rules of a video game, and I know that my goal is to locate and rescue students while avoiding a fire, but with each repetition, just as a map of the corridors germinates in my thoughts, and the location of the fire and the voices become clear, the film plot introduces another nuance: I hear a troupe of footfalls, of hard bootheels on linoleum, and I know that stomping is the police. I don't know whether the police are chasing me or whether they're looking for the students. I do know that if the police stumble upon me they will arrest me before I reach the students, and if they reach the students first, they will swing their truncheons before making arrests.

I start to navigate the corridors with an ear to the students, an ear to the police footfalls, and a wariness of the fire. The film introduces another complication: the corridors fill with smoke. To avoid suffocating I have to proceed on my knees, crawling through the corridors while holding my lapel over my nose and mouth.

On my knees in the corridors, the students' voices get lost in the smoke. I can no longer locate the footsteps. I know that I can't outwit the police, the smoke, the labyrinthine corridor, that it will gradually entrap me. I also know that the film is not an adventure, but an ungainly hybrid of psychological thriller, horror, and historical documentary informed by an episode that remains unresolved, and, unless I can resolve the episode outside of the film, I will forever be trapped inside the vertiginous narrative. My objective then becomes to escape the narrative before it ensnares me.

Every December a small shoot of worry insinuates itself into my days. I think ahead to February, and I worry that it may be my last year to make the hybrid documentary, and that if I don't do it, one of two scenarios will arise: someone else will produce a film in their own fashion, or the episode will be collectively forgotten. Either way, my own aesthetic reckoning with that moment will never be expressed. I worry about the intensity of my obsession. A third scenario presents itself: what if I make a poor film? I know nothing about film. I don't watch movies, and I have never practiced any of the arts. I don't know how to think about plot. Some years a traditional plot, with its rising action, climax, and dénoument, suggests itself, while other years it expands in an infinite and exhausting maze. On January 29th, the day the Concordia Computer Center was occupied in 1969, dreams begin. They intensify until February 11th, when they reach their peak, then they disperse. Their dispersal coincides with a release from any desire for recognition at Cannes, or any feelings of urgency about making the film.

This past January I returned from a visit to Senegal, where I bought a wooden elephant from an outdoor market. The elephant's body was hollowed out, and according to the craftsman it could be used to store human ashes, money, dreams, regrets, juju, jewelry, memory, anything I wanted. I placed the elephant in the center of my dining table, and often before I went to sleep I would look at it, taking a drink of water, and it would be the last thing in my thoughts before I drifted off.

Most days I was groggy and depleted by my late night contemplation of the film. It often felt like I was walking around in a haze. The haze could thin out to reveal reality or it could become subtle hallucinations. I might look up from my copy of the *Contract*, a near unreadable Caribbean community paper in which I advertise my shop and my goods, and which I pick up as a habit and spread out on the counter, and the faces of people in the newspaper might resemble the masks on my wall, and vice versa. Or, out of the corner of my eye, the spindly statues that stand around the store might shift position. They might lift a leg, move a few steps to the left, or turn their heads to face the door. When I looked back at them they would be standing immobile. Or I might be in the middle of reading an article when the words would sound in my thoughts like they were being spoken, and for a moment voices would seem to issue from my statues and masks. People might enter my store and ask me a question in English, and I might answer in Wolof.

The hallucinations were worse this past year than in any previous year, so when I saw a picture of one of my regular customers—Tamika Brown—in the *Contract*, I thought my mind was producing the illusion. Tamika visited the store at least once a week on her way to and from Concordia. She assertively bargained but never bought anything. I closed the paper, then walked around the store and muttered the name "Tamika Brown" three times, thinking that if I invoked her by repeating her name, any imposter spirit would be frightened away.

I opened the *Contract* again to the same page, and the picture of Tamika was still there, so I glanced down at the article to see if it was readable, or if its sentences turned into snakes:

Local Scholar Awarded Grant to Research Grenadian History

I kept wondering whether my mind was inventing the article as I went, and I kept blinking, squinting, waiting for the lines of type to wriggle. They didn't.

I was doubly surprised when Tamika wandered into the store. She smiled at me. I squinted again. I put on my glasses and looked down at the paper and then back at her. Tamika paused, then asked me if I was alright.

Euh, oui, oui, euh, juste un peu étourdi ma chère.

"Dizzy? How come?"

Je manque de sommeil, c'est tout, and I made up an excuse, *depuis mon retour du Sénégal le décalage me dérange. Ça ira mieux dans quelques jours.*

"I hear you. I was totally jet lagged on my last trip to Sénégal. It took about a week to get back to normal. You'll get through it."

Still, I tilted my glasses to the edge of my nose, and stared down at the photo in the *Contract*, then back at Tamika as she browsed. Both versions of Tamika, the print version and the flesh, continued to exist simultaneously. We discussed the price of a wooden giraffe and, as usual, couldn't find a mutually satisfactory figure, so she browsed the necklaces and amulets in silence, and I offered, *si tu trouves quelque chose que tu aimes, je peux te faire un prix.* She thanked me, continued browsing, then waved as she wandered out. I returned to the article.

Local Scholar Awarded Grant to Research Grenadian History

BY CONTRACT STAFF

Local Scholar Tamika Brown was recently awarded the prestigious CLR James Caribbean Research Grant. The grant is for international scholars, but it is only awarded for projects that focus on Caribbean history. Tamika Brown is the first female recipient and the first Canadian. She recently sat down with *Contract* staff to discuss her success and her research.

Contract staff: So, Tamika, congratulations are in order. What are you going to do with the money?

Tamika Brown: Well, the money is earmarked for research-related expenses. I had to submit a budget to the foundation, which they studied and approved. My research involves travel to visit university archives, libraries, galleries, community centers, to purchase equipment with which to interview people, and to visit other cultural archives in the Caribbean region.

Contract staff: So, your research is about Grenada?

Tamika Brown: Yes, it's about the Grenada revolution specifically, but more broadly it's about the revolution's regional resonance. In this case, regional means throughout the Caribbean. I am very interested in exploring what impact the New Jewel Movement and its manifesto had on similarly minded organizations in other islands. One parallel is the state-orchestrated murder of Walter Rodney in Guyana one year after the NJM succeeded in seizing power in Grenada. That—

Contract Staff: Are you jumping to some conclusions Ms. Brown?

Tamika Brown: About what?

Contract Staff: Well, foremost that the revolution had any resonance across the region, and then that the Rodney incident was indeed state-orchestrated.

Tamika Brown: I've already done enough research to substantiate both of those claims.

Contract Staff: Which we at the *Contract* haven't seen and can't confirm ourselves. And yes, what we want to focus on here is your research. So, please tell our readers, when does your work begin?

Tamika Brown: As I was just saying, it's already begun, it's ongoing, and it has already substantiated that the revolution's impact was not limited to Grenada alone.

Contract Staff: And how does it feel to be the first woman, and the first Canadian to achieve this prestigious academic distinction?

Tamika Brown: I think it's far too late in the 21st century for there to continue to be firsts like this. Let's break down the barriers. At the same time, it is an honor, but I think of it less as a personal honor and more as a valuation of the work, and of the fact that there are people who want to know more about the revolution and its impact.

Contract Staff: Certainly. Thank you Ms. Brown. We wish you success with your research, and God bless.

That night I researched Tamika Brown online. I found a paper she wrote as a graduate student at Concordia, on the 40th anniversary of the 1969 occupation of the computer center. She referenced maps of the 9th floor of the Hall Building, maps from 1969, before any renovations had been made, in which she pinpointed where the students had barricaded themselves into the computer center, where the police were stationed, and where the fires were lit. The students were blamed for lighting the fires, and the newspapers reported this. Yet, on being arrested, many students admitted to vandalizing university property, and tossing boxes of punchcards out a smashed window. Tamika's paper stressed, however, that the students refused to accept responsibility for smashing the computers or lighting the fires. Many students even claimed that the police themselves smashed the computers to intimidate the students and exaggerate the extent of the damage (a tactic that would increase the charges laid) and that the police also lit the fires. The paper notes that the fires were lit in a place that blocked the most convenient route to the escalators and stairs. The escalators and the stairs, the two means of escape, were then accessible by one circuitous route, which traveled the narrow corridors that curved outside the computer center, then bent back behind a lecture hall, and re-emerged on the other wing of the floor, where the police were conveniently stationed. Tamika's paper goes on to examine several different scenarios related to the fires and the arrests. Perhaps a police collaborator was planted among the students, perhaps the students lit the fire without having contemplated an exit strategy, etc. The paper proposes, through an analysis of these various options, and insight gleaned from statements made by the students who were arrested, that the police were responsible for the most costly vandalism and arson.

I fell asleep reading Tamika's paper. I dreamed that I was on the set of my film, with her paper crumpled in my jacket pocket. I was navigating the 9th floor corridors. In my dream I knew what was going to happen to the students, and I knew who lit the fire, but I still couldn't do anything about it. That knowing made the dream burn. The corridors sweltered, the police footsteps charged, the smoke swelled, and I was near frantic in my search. I knew the students would be arrested and beaten, and when I finally had to crawl beneath the gathering smoke, I choked and coughed, and felt myself losing consciousness on the linoleum. I woke up sweating, and I sat up in the dark and almost wept when the dream finally dissipated. But even as it dissipated it seemed to leave a dark dye in my thoughts, and that dye seeped down through me. I got up, and as I flipped on the light in the kitchen I saw the elephant.

Its wood gleamed black. I stared at the elephant, that majestic long-memoried animal, and then I opened the compartment on its back. It was hollowed out. I left the compartment open and I allowed my memory to travel back to 1969. I had just returned from a failed covert engagement in Lausanne, and my employer, my employer who was the government of Québec, a nation struggling to determine its identity and its future, just like many of the nations in Africa and the Caribbean, offered me the chance to redeem myself in its eyes. I summoned this memory and poured it into the elephant.

I recalled office numbers, the names of government officers and their precise titles, I recalled who smoked cigarettes and who didn't, and I recalled the brands. I recalled whose office had windows and whose occupied a corner. I recalled who drove a brown Datsun, who drove a chrome Peugeot, and who drove a compact gold FIAT. I recalled exact conversations and poured them, in their entirety, into the elephant.

I recalled being tasked to infiltrate the student movement. I recalled looking at building plans of the 9th floor, at the layout of the narrow labyrinthine corridors, the passage that traveled behind the lecture hall, the location of the stairs and the escalator. I was instructed on how to pressure the students to more radical action, and to push them toward a criminal blunder. I recalled the names of the men who encouraged me and the exact words they used, and I poured all of that sepia-toned nostalgia into the elephant.

I recalled being told that the specifics of this engagement could only be detailed verbally, and could not be written down. I also recalled a particular Montréal police captain who was present at each of these meetings, I recalled the exact circumference of his stomach, and I recalled his remark that it was good to have *un bon black de notre côté*, a good black on our side, which made the other officers laugh, and which he thought I didn't hear. I delivered all of those memories to the elephant.

I recalled attending the student meetings and revealing what my employer had requested of me, and then returning to my employer and delivering a mix of accurate information and falsehoods as subtle as the narrow winding corridors that gradually clouded a person's sense of direction, in the same way that the back streets of the Old Port did, or the convoluted neural pathways a memory travels as it is recalled, misleading, directionless falsehoods about what the students were planning. I recalled this deliberate, duplicitous crossing of the hemispheres, north and south, and I told it all to the elephant.

Finally, I recalled the meeting at which I was asked to set a fire on the 9th floor, and I said that I would do it. After the meeting I went to stand outside the Hall Building on de Maisonneuve Boulevard. It was the middle of February, and I looked up to the 9th floor and hoped that the students would be safe, and I knew they would be herded to their arrest, that they might be beaten and insulted, and instead of entering the Hall building to light the fire, I vanished into the city. I walked along de Maisonneuve Boulevard until I found the entrance to the Peel metro tunnel, and I rode the escalator underground. I gave all of this to the elephant, in all of its detail. I recalled the exact number of snowflakes that fell that day, and the faces of the people I passed on the street. I remembered everything, and once I delivered it to the elephant, I closed the compartment.

I planned to give the elephant to the historian, with a word of caution. It contained a memory, and if it were opened, that memory would rush out like a swarm of bats in the dusk of Dakar.

Smoke that Thundered

I HEARD VOICES YELLING over the water's roar. Their timbre was familiar, their urgent inflection tugged at something inside me. A thump resounded in the middle of my chest, where a moment ago it was silent, and that thump became insistent, articulate. It told me to kick out my feet, which I did. I kicked out. I twisted, trying to fling my hand toward the voices. A knot tightened in my chest, like a stifled breath, and my body seemed to wrench toward the voices. I recognized my name echoing out amid the rush of white noise and the gurgle of the river in the rocks, and then I didn't hear anything. I was submerged, as if the entire brown river, the Potaro River in Guyana, were a ribbon of magnetic tape, and my body was a sound trapped in its warble, twisting, being warped by the dubmaster, my own scream distorted into a squawk of feedback. Then I was back up, bobbing and gasping. I heard my name shouted out: Kaie! Kaie!

Growing up, my name was something I disliked more than school. Nobody else at any school I ever attended had a name like mine. I preferred more common names, like Kelly because of its athletic roll, or Jay because it seemed to flit. Chris flew off the tongue, and if I were Chris I might acquire the properties of that name and be sleek, nimble, and sought after. Around that time my parents introduced me to *Roots* by Alex Haley. Early in the story, the newborn Kunta Kinte undergoes a naming ceremony. His name is imbued with meaning, ancestry, and spiritual resonance. If someone inherited that name in Calgary circa 1986, they'd be ridiculed. No ceremony could change that.

I didn't finish the book. I understood that I was born here, in the suburbs of southwest Calgary, that we owned a 3,000-square-foot house, two cars, and I had "everything." My children now have everything. The purpose of making me read *Roots* was to teach me humility. The point was that people born in other circumstances persevere and live richly with less. A byproduct of my reading was that I became doubly sensitive to my name, which features in South American Indigenous myth. Kaie was an Arawak chief who paddled his canoe over a waterfall in a sacrifice to Makunaima, the creator, to assure his people's future. I always withheld that story when people asked me about my name, because Calgarians despise Indians.

One of my uncles disputed the story of Chief Kaie and Makunaima. My parents dismissed his alternate versions as cynicism. He dismissed the myth as a fiction of patriotism, or a fable to lift the hearts of children and the credulous. He annoyed everyone by asserting that the real legend is about an irascible old man who drank too much high wine, went out on the Potaro River in his canoe, but he was too drunk to control the canoe, and his canoe sailed over the falls, and since then the falls have been known as Kaie Teur Falls, which means Old Man Falls.

I don't know which legend is true. Maybe Chief Kaie had to drink high wines to imbue himself with enough courage to paddle over the falls. Maybe his people put him in the canoe and sent him over the falls because they blamed him for their hardships, or they did it because he was cantankerous and insufferable. Maybe he hated his name so much that he decided to throw himself over the falls, or he was simply tired of living. Maybe he was too old to continue being an effective chief, and rather than dishonor himself and his people, he chose a more noble and dramatic exit. Whatever the case, I still think about it. I even dream about it. The dream dissipates in the mornings so I can never completely remember it, but I wake up gasping, to a chorus of voices shouting: Kaie! Kaie!

The Calgarians stood out in Pearson Airport. They wore decorative belt buckles, bolo ties, and cowboy hats. Flush-faced men, they waddled through security while discussing last night's hockey game. Their presence in Pearson, by the Caribbean Airlines gates, was a reminder that although I might leave the city of Calgary, I would always carry its culture with me. Flying over the United States, and then down in an arc to land in Port of Spain, Trinidad, the Calgarians dissected the features of the latest Ford F-series pickup truck. Likely they were on their way to a resort where they would lie on the beach and further discuss the Oilers, the Flames, and their competing chances for success in the NHL playoffs. I've always been ambivalent about beaches, but my ambivalence sours when I consider playoffs, cowboy attire, and pickup trucks.

One morning I was crossing a street on my way to Bishop Pinkham Junior High School. A driver revved his engine just as I passed in front of his pickup. I stopped—startled—and he gunned his engine again. I glowered at him, still standing in front of the chrome grille of his pickup, and he leaned out the window and snapped, "Git along, boy." I looked at my reflection in the polished grille, then across at the curb, where I noticed a stone, about the size of a lime. I bolted, scooped the stone in my hand, pivoted, launched the stone at his door, and sprinted off. The stone struck his door with a brief metallic *ching*, and I shivered with delight and fear. Then I heard his voice, hoarse, raised. I shivered again as I ran. I looked back and he was halfway out of his truck, but he just stood there, one leg on the ground and the other on the polished running board, a perm hanging over his collar. I stopped, gave him the finger, then ducked into an alley.

As I walked I glanced through the slats in fences. I saw swing sets and tree houses, landscaped yards, stone patios and patio sets, umbrellas and awnings, the familiar accessories we had in our backyard, the things my mother thought about when she told us that we had everything. I took a long detour through alleys and up side streets. I smoked a cigarette as I walked. I got to school late, and when I arrived I was instantly called to the office.

I knew enough to anticipate heat. My parents told me that the Caribbean and South America were not dry like the prairies, that the air was moist. They also told me I would be going to a place where everyone was Black and Brown, and that it would be very different from Calgary. I looked across the aisle at Uncle Koffi, whose head lolled back, his mouth open but silent as he slept.

Once in Trinidad we'd transfer to a smaller plane that would fly us to Timehri International Airport in Georgetown, Guyana. I was going somewhere I'd never been before, somewhere I was supposedly from, and that word, "from," carried unspecified expectations, although the force of inflection told me that "from" assumed a connection, one that I was expected to feel and to further establish.

What if I didn't feel a connection? I didn't know what I was supposed to feel when I arrived. I was told to relax, be myself, and fit in, but it didn't make sense, because just by being myself I'd become a problem, which was why I was being sent to Guyana in the first place. I thought of my being sent elsewhere as a way to solve the problem of the person I was becoming in Calgary. The idea seemed to be that I couldn't know myself until I encountered myself in Guyana. My parents thought I would "develop" when I was there. Again another ambiguous word: from, develop, connection. The meaning of those common words was shifted by my having become who I was without having visited Guyana. What if the trip had no effect?

One of Uncle Koffi's relatives was meeting us at the airport. My mom went to Bishops with his sisters when they were growing up in Georgetown. Uncle Koffi said that all of his relatives had heard of me and wanted to meet me. I didn't know any of them, and I hoped there weren't too many. On the plane it occurred to me that I might be expected to share a room or participate in activities. Why hadn't this occurred to me earlier? I would likely be expected to show gratitude. I might even be made to feel indebted. I instantly resented Uncle Koffi's relatives, and just for feeling that thin needle of resentment, I worried that I might be punished with church.

I had last been to a church three years before, the Catholic church by John Ware Junior High. Before that I'd never been to church in any consistent way. At the time I'd been punished with an unfair and unmerited suspension from school. I was sitting in class, idly staring into the schoolyard, when a boy with a haircut like mine, a flat-top fade, turned onto a path that cut through the yard. He was smoking a cigarette.

At the same time, and unbeknownst to me, one of the teachers in another class saw the same boy and called the office. I saw the boy drop his cigarette and start running. He glanced over his shoulder, swerved off the path, and sprinted toward some trees. I lost sight of him. I wondered what he was running from. Moments later I saw the vice-principal rush outside and intently search the yard. The VP walked the perimeter of the school, growing more and more indignant, and by the time he returned to his office, the periods had changed. He phoned my new class. The teacher answered, paused, then said: "Yes he's here," while looking directly at me. Once she got off the phone she told me: "Kaie, you are expected in the office," in front of the class. The other students said: "Oooooooo," and I echoed: "Oooooooo". I left the class amid laughter.

The VP asked me where I was during my previous class. I told him I was in class. He asked me again. I told him the same thing. We kept repeating the exchange, circling one another. I had no idea why I was there or what he was suggesting, so I said, "this is bullshit," and insisted on going back to class. He was livid. He called my mother and told her a teacher had seen me smoking outside of school when I should have been in class, and that I was using profanity in his office.

My mother hurried out of work to meet with the VP. By the time she arrived I convinced the VP to check with my 2nd period science teacher, who confirmed that I had indeed been in class, and another boy, wearing clothes different from mine, had been smoking outside the school. The VP sent me to a Calgary Board of Education counselor, where I continued to demand an apology that I never received. I did receive a three-day suspension for using hostile language. After that I became so belligerent that my parents entrusted me to the church.

I was dressed up in brown pressed slacks, a yellow Lacoste wool sweater, and a shirt and tie underneath, then dropped off at the Catholic church by John Ware School. I still wonder why my mother didn't accompany me, because I had never attended a Catholic service, whereas she went to Catholic schools in Guyana. Apparently the John Ware School was named after a Black cowboy who had been enslaved in South Carolina in the 1800s, and who first introduced cattle and ranching to Alberta. I can't help myself. I have to ask if that means Alberta owes its culture and its prosperity to a formerly enslaved man, a migrant from the US via Africa? I don't know, any more than I knew then when to stand up, sing, speak, or sit down, so I sat in silence and observed the Catholic ceremony. At the opposite end of my pew, two middle-aged women glowered in my direction. Outside after the service, a freckled blond boy left his mother's side and taunted me with, "hey nigger." I knocked him down and wrestled myself on top of him, but he grinned. His braces gleamed. He taunted me again, saying that his dad just paid two thousand dollars for his new braces, and if I damaged them his parents would sue me.

I winced as I punched him in the mouth. His braces slipped off his teeth and snarled his upper lip. Blood appeared. He howled. I whispered: "Shut up, shut up." He wouldn't, so I shouted at him. I told him I would kill him if he didn't shut up. He bawled louder, and just as I was raising my arm again, two women grabbed me. My mother was there, yanking me free and rebuking the women. The church crowd stood back and watched.

The final solution, for which my parents consulted four other families, the Nascimentos, the Mohabirs, the Changs, and the Dos Ramoses, was to send me to Guyana. I didn't know what that meant, but I knew I would likely be in church with Uncle Koffi's family. I hoped I could extract myself from it, but somehow, I doubted so because every Guyanese person we knew went to a Catholic church.

The roar of the engines and the rush of air outside the cabin numbed my ears. My eyelids drooped and my neck relaxed. As I drifted, the noise became rushing water. I was standing up to my knees in coppery water, with the sunlight shimmering along its surface. Several meters in front of me the water surged over broad black rocks and tumbled down, foaming as it fell, its mist rising like smoke and moistening the canopy that itself seemed to froth and bubble green. As the water tumbled an electric charge drew me forward, and I felt myself dissolving into the current.

Uncle Koffi was shaking my shoulder gently and saying my name across the aisle. "Kaie, time to wake up, we're about to touch down in Trinidad."

Inside Piarco International Airport we sat facing tall windows that overlooked the runway. Yellow fields sprawled into green, which rolled to the horizon, where bush arose and palms bent in the wind. A mist rose off the asphalt, off the yellow fields, off the green. It seemed that the moisture and coolness of the night was being sucked up toward the sun, and once it had all evaporated, the sun would beat against the blue, the green, the yellow, the black asphalt, and the island itself would blaze with heat and life.

"Boy, Trinidad's hot," my uncle shook his head, "but Guyana is South, between the ocean and the Amazon. It's a different kind of heat you feel there." Uncle Koffi sat back smiling. I stared out the window and watched as the mist cleared.

Another plane landed. Parents filed off with their children. Everyone was disheveled and shiny-faced from the hot flight. I wondered whether they were returning from England, Miami, or New York, or whether some of them were like me, from a remote corner of the Commonwealth and visiting home for the first time. I listened to the boys my age who spoke in a quickened clip, and not with the flattened tone of Canadian English, and I realized that I might be perceived as having an accent. I felt momentarily displaced, like I was observing myself from the outside.

"Are you hungry? Do you feel for a snack?" My uncle's voice was shifting. His vowels were tightening, shortening, while his consonants sounded with more snap. Before I could answer he was walking over to a kiosk at which an Indian woman was sitting, her form framed by a display of soda pop, plantain chips, and sweets, all brands I'd never seen before. The woman smiled easily at my uncle and they started talking. He laughed, his body loose and fluid, and their voices bounced back and forth, sharing the same cadence, their gestures mirroring one another.

My uncle seemed strange to me, different from the man I knew. He fit in here, he understood the rhythm and he could speak the language, whereas I could not. I realized how attached to him I was. I needed his help to navigate the people, the language, but I was also estranged. I was seeing the emergence of another person whom he hid inside himself when he was in Calgary. The person he was when in Calgary, the familiar uncle, seemed to recede. I was different. I knew that no other person existed inside me. No other would emerge fully formed, laughing and bantering in another language, leaning casually against a pillar in the airport lounge while the day rose over Trinidad, a day in which that person held a place. I looked back out at the mist, still rising over the yellow and green, swimming up and dissipating in the blue, and I thought that perhaps all of my relatives were haunted like my uncle. They were haunted by other selves, people they had spent lifetimes cultivating. When they were in Calgary they were haunted by their Guyanese selves, and when they were in Georgetown, or Port of Spain, they were haunted by their Canadian selves.

I wondered how it felt to be so haunted. Was it painful? Was it something that influenced their dreams or... and then I thought that it might be like what I was feeling in the airport, like the self with whom I had grown familiar, the person I thought was simply my natural being, "me," was not wholly me but was just a version that I shouldn't become too attached to, that I shouldn't become confined by, and perhaps I was other than the character who performed the speech, gestures, and accepted behavior of Calgary, and I could adapt my performance to the culture of Trinidad or Guyana if I needed to. My uncle passed me a patty, a banana, and a bottle of water.

The white noise thundered in my ears again as we flew over the strip of water that separated Trinidad from the South American mainland. The noise quieted as the plane rolled to a stop in front of Timehri International Airport. We filed down an aluminum staircase onto the landing.

The air pressed against my body and then drew back, as if sucking at it, pulling the pores open and inviting my skin to breathe with it. My uncle leaned in to me and said: "You feel that? Three degrees below sea level, bwoy. Three degrees below sea level, and to the south, the rainforest. That's what you're feeling." We walked with our carry-on luggage toward a little building that looked more like a 19th-century New England inn than an airport. It was painted cream with ochre trim. We queued up for customs.

Security agents stood against the walls. Customs officers sat in little booths and processed the travelers. Dark skin gleamed. The womens' hair was pulled back and tied up in buns that sat atop their heads, and they spoke more slowly than the people in Trinidad, and with a slight lilt that recalled the speech of my parents, aunts, uncles, grandparents. Uncle Koffi was humming to himself, rocking back on his heels and forward on his tiptoes. When we reached the customs booth the agent took our passports. Uncle Koffi confirmed that we were traveling together, and that I was his nephew. The woman then asked the purpose of our visit, and my uncle said: "Family visit, and to introduce this young one to his roots." The woman said: "Welcome to Guyana, please enjoy your stay," and her glance angled down and took me in, included me, and carried me through customs and into the baggage claim area, where people reunited with relatives, argued about baggage, and talked more freely now that they were officially admitted.

I waited a full hour in the school office, and when the principal called me in, he went quiet and stared at me.

"Do you know why you're here?"

"No." I met his gaze for a few seconds. It felt like he was trying to see something inside me, to open me up, reach into me and extract my thoughts, and when he refused to look away I felt his wilfulness. His face was firm, his lips pulled into a flat line. I decided to focus on a single thought, to will it to materialize in the air between us. I thought: I can anticipate you.

He asked me again, "Do you know why you're here?"

"No." We stared at each other. "Why am I here?"

"You don't have any idea why you're here?"

"If I came of my own will I would know, but I didn't."

"Don't be clever with me."

"Do you mind telling me why I'm here?"

The principal, sighing, took off his glasses and leaned back. He continued to contemplate me. His voice softened. "Do you recall anything... unusual from this morning?"

I paused, wary of his softened tone. "I got to class a bit late because I took a detour. It took longer than expected."

"Oh, you took a detour, of course." He still sounded sly, like he knew something that I didn't. "And why did you take that detour?" He leaned forward again.

Inwardly I groaned as I recalled the pickup truck, the rock, the permed man with one foot on the running board. Had the man followed me to school? How could he have? I went in the opposite direction, turning down alleys and side streets. Had he driven past the school and glimpsed me walking in? I decided to admit, but also to assert myself. "Because a grown man in a pickup truck revved his engine at me as I was crossing the street, then leaned out the window and insulted me for no reason. I didn't want to come across another person like that, so I took a detour."

The principal's eyes tightened. "So, someone in a truck *threatened* you at an intersection?" He stretched out the word, as if questioning its veracity while questioning my commitment to the statement.

"Yes." I described the pickup and the person in it. I told him exactly how the man revved his engine twice, then leaned out his window and said, "Git along, boy."

"Mm-hmm." The principal maintained his sly tone. "Are you certain that's what happened?"

I repeated the incident word for word, and then I added, "This isn't the first time. Usually when it happens the driver calls me a racial name."

"Well that didn't happen this time, did it?"

"No, it didn't."

"Then why would you bring it up? Are you trying to make an accusation of some sort?"

I thought about what I was going to say next. He was wearing square tortoiseshell glasses that were too broad for his face. They magnified his eyes. "No. I just made a comparison. Why would anyone rev their engine at someone they don't know, then lean out the window and insult them? It doesn't make any sense, but it has happened to me before. That's what I'm saying."

He dropped his point. "Did you recognize that man at all?"

"No. I've never seen him before."

"Are you sure?"

"Yes."

"Are you sure you've never seen him before?"

"I just told you that."

"Fine. And did you do anything after the man leaned out of his truck and told you to git along?"

"'Git along *boy.*'"

"As you wish. 'Git along *boy.*'"

"It isn't what I wish, it's what was said."

"Fine."

"Yes, I threw a rock at his truck and then ran. I turned around and gave him the finger. He got out of the truck like he wanted to chase me."

"Are you sure that's what happened?"

"I can write it down for you if you want."

"Well you just might have to, because that man is a

teacher at this school. Mr. Manning. He teaches mathematics. Now are you sure you've never seen him before?"

That surprised me. The principal opened his office door, then motioned for someone to enter. A moment later, the man with a collar-length brown perm, mustache, and brown glasses was standing in the doorway.

"Is this the man you saw this morning," the principal asked, emphasizing "this" with a rising inflection.

"Yes, that's him. Thank you for bringing him in here so I could identify him. I'd like to press charges."

Mr. Manning opened his mouth and took in air, and his eyes widened like they wanted to take in air as well, but the principal ushered him out.

"Thank you Mr. Manning, that's enough." He closed the door. "I don't think you understand how serious this is. This isn't the moment to be joking around."

"I'm not joking. That man threatened me on my way to school. I am a boy, he is a man. He was in a truck. I was on foot. If he's a teacher at this school, even though I've never seen him here before, he should get fired. Teachers shouldn't threaten students."

"You know, Kaie, this isn't the first time you've been in this office. And frankly, we're not here to discuss Mr. Manning." The principal punctuated his statement by adjusting his brown blazer, as he entwined his fingers atop his desk. "We're here to discuss you and your conduct."

"In this situation I didn't act alone, so I think we have to discuss that teacher's conduct too."

"Mr. Manning is a colleague of mine, an *esteemed* colleague, and I find it very hard to believe that he would aggress you for no reason. I also find it quite hard to believe you, given your history of being disruptive. There was the recent fistfight with Stephen—"

"He attacked me. I didn't have a choice."

"There is always a choice. Last week there was the incident where you spoke back to your chemistry teacher."

"I didn't appreciate his tone."

"And in September there was the incident with the orange that you threw across the street, which could have struck someone and done serious harm."

"Yes, and do you remember what the shop teacher said to me? He called me an asshole in front of the other students. He isn't supposed to be swearing at students. What's wrong with you people?"

"My point, Kaie, is that your disruptiveness seems to be a pattern, and it doesn't seem to be something that you are trying to control. It includes profanity and even acts of violence, which I can't condone. I'm going to ask you to sit outside," he sighed, "and once again we'll be in contact with your parents."

At the house in Republic Park, my Auntie Shanice kept after me to do chores. Unless I was reading, I was expected to dry the dishes, sweep the veranda, fold the laundry. I had brought *The Hichhiker's Guide to the Galaxy* with me, but found it too convoluted. On a rattan bookshelf that matched all of the furniture in the family room, I saw the title *L'esclave vieil homme et le molosse*. It was in French, and due to my French immersion program at school, I could understand some sections.

The book, *Slave Old Man and the Mastiff*, was about an old man in Martinique who had been a slave since birth. He had managed, through a combination of compliance, work, and resilience, to reach a position of relative respect on his sugar plantation. He worked independently and had no fear of being abused.

Something happened. I'm not sure what, because I didn't understand all of the passages, but he was running away from his plantation, and his owners loosed a young mastiff after him. The mastiff was muscled, aggressive, and known to be a relentless pursuer of fugitives. As the old man ran he entered the jungle. The jungle seemed to have a magical effect on him, and it recalled his youth and his entire life to him. As he ran, his mind traveled back through the streaks of green. His legs grew hard and his stride limber again. He gained speed and became an emanation of the forest's intelligence. He knew its paths as it guided him back through his own life.

I left the book in the car that morning. We drove to the small airport and took a Cessna out to Kaieteur National Park. The Cessna shuddered with each gust of wind, but out the window, green burst and rippled to the horizon in every direction, the sky a searing blue above. The Cessna landed on an airstrip, and an Arawak guide led us into the jungle. As we crossed into denser foliage I sensed rustlings in all directions, eyes blinking between leaves, immobile insects watching, everything alive. I imagined broad fronds closing behind me.

Sunlight broke between the leaves and streamed down. Branches interwove, and high overhead I heard cries, some of which sounded like laughter. I wanted to laugh too, but I didn't know if the sounds were made by birds or monkeys. I wanted to call out to them. I had a sense that they had names, which I ought to know. I felt an impulse to plunge deeper into the forest, to disappear into it.

I pictured myself running along what seemed to be a magnetic ribbon. It unspooled as I placed one foot down in front of the other. The ribbon—the path—was bunched and winding. The path looked like damp, hammered copper. The shapes of leaves and fronds overlapping formed its layered design. It wound between trees, under roots that had broken the soil. Fallen branches lay across it, and in places it forked off in different directions.

Birds flew at eye-level, zipping through the foliage, streaking color behind them, neon trails fading into the air.

I ran, treading on the soft limbs of ferns living quietly in the shade, slapping branches aside. I ran with my hands in front of my face to deflect any leaf-burdened living thing that might slash my eye, or my cheek, inadvertently kicking the carcasses of fallen fruits, swarmed by ants, into the bush, the fruits spinning like planets dashed out of their orbit.

I ran, and over my breath, which heaved up into my ears, over the dumb weight of my heels on the moist mosaic of leaves, over the rustlings of lizards whose alerted eyes swiveled in their orbital sockets, over the cries and the breaking flap of birds, I heard a faint but constant hiss.

As I ran, the hiss opened into a roar. It seemed to arise from somewhere inside the earth, and I knew that if I kept along the path I would meet its source. I ran toward the roar.

Behind me, in the distance of my memory was Georgetown and the gated three-story house in Republic Park where I'd been staying with Uncle Koffi. Everyone pronounced his name Cuffy, and even I had adopted that pronunciation. The house belonged to his sister, my Auntie Shanice, who had studied music at the University of the West Indies and later at Juilliard. When she eventually returned to Guyana she founded her own music school that catered to the elite students of the region. Children of government ministers were sent from Trinidad, Barbados, and Jamaica to study with her. Her home was full of instruments: a white Wurlitzer piano, violins, trumpets, two King Super 20 tenor saxophones, and acoustic guitars which I strummed idly. I had nothing else to do, because every time I tried to leave the house with my cousins, someone warned, "Kaie! Be careful," and "Kaie! Make sure you be careful," and they firmly instructed my cousins to watch out for me. Whenever we left the house we had to drive, and being out after dark was forbidden. When night fell the crickets sounded a hiss that rose from the ground up to the veranda above the car port. Frogs and lizards interwove with the hiss, overlapped, and made it impossible to dwell in silence.

I couldn't sleep because of the heat and the insects. I was watched so closely that I never managed to slip outside for a cigarette. I secretively asked one of my cousins if I could go out of the gates for a smoke. He was so appalled by my smoking that I worried he would tell his parents. I never brought it up again. When my cousins were together they would speak Creole, of which I only understood fragments, and as they spoke they side-eyed me.

I couldn't bear to listen to my aunts, uncles, and their friends, who, drinking Banks beer in the air-conditioned kitchen, recounted stories of expatriates who returned after years abroad, only to be robbed on their way in from the airport; successful retirees murdered in home invasions; students back from studies in England kidnapped and held for ransom. After dinner each night I exiled myself to the veranda with the novel about the old slave and the mastiff. I took breaks from my reading to strum the few chords my Auntie Shanice taught me, on an old Washburn acoustic guitar. In my tuneless strumming I fell into daydreams about Calgary. I dreamed of carefree bicycle rides by the Glenmore Reservoir, the dirt path that zigzagged through the tall yellow grass, of smoking a joint down on the rocks while watching the sunlight ripple on the water.

As I ran, insects scattered upward and hid on the undersides of leaves. The tall house in Republic Park receded, as did that morning's flight over the rainforest in a dragonfly-blue Cessna. The small plane trembled as it swung beneath the clouds. We stared out its fogged windows at the sprawling green, the green foaming to the horizon in every direction. All of the claustrophobia and stress of Georgetown receded, along with the gated houses and spooled razorwire, the green canefields and brown rivers bending into the interior and receding in my memory at the same time.

The Cessna dipped between mountains and below cloud. Light rain speckled the windows, and the plane leveled down toward an airstrip. A few feet from the airstrip stood a wooden house where we met a brown man with a wide nose and eyes slanted upward, who led us down a path into the jungle. The path was damp, the color of dark copper. As I followed it I felt it move. It shifted— slithered—under my feet. With each step I felt it shift, as if it wished to carry me somewhere, and I was compelled to run.

I ran.

The roar grew louder, and raindrops slipped through the vegetation as if riding beams of light to the ground. I felt my heart surge in my eardrums, in time to my feet on the path. The roar seemed to rise up from the center of the earth. I broke through the trees into a clearing. I slid on rain-slicked rocks and managed to steady myself. The Potaro River, brown, wide, and slow-moving, poured its tons of water over jagged rocks. The water appeared to hover for a moment, and to go golden-white, then to tumble down in a torrent. I waded into the warm river. The current tugged gently at my ankles.

I went in up to my knees, stopped, and stared out to where the water was launched over the falls. It fell with a magnetic intensity. The falls tugged me forward.

I waded in up to my thighs. A line of birds disappeared over the treeline of the opposite bank. Something inside me—a resistance to water, an instinct to remain dry— dissolved, and I felt an urge to completely liquefy into the river. That furious point at which the water tumbled over the rocks seemed smooth, and I kept seeing myself gliding, birdlike, through the water and over the edge, becoming the water itself as I fell, becoming that smoke that thundered. I waded in up to my waist, and the current's heavy drag tugged at me, but my feet were firm on the riverbed's firm stones. I heard my name in the torrent of water—I thought I heard it. The water was speaking.

"Kaie."

But then its voice became submerged in noise before it rose back up and uttered, "Kaie," faintly, and I waded in up to my chest. In a demonstration of its power, the current raised me off my feet and gently set me down a second later. I wasn't afraid of it.

"Kaie."

I wasn't afraid of the rocks at the edge of the falls; they were smooth. I closed my eyes and waded farther in. The water rushed around my neck, and my feet kept being lifted off the riverbed and set back down.

"Kaie."

The voice was closer to me, and somehow more frantic.

"Kaie."

I lowered myself under the golden surface of the river.

Notes of a Hand

I AM THIS AMANUENSIS, this hand, this ghost, this slave. I am in the story while being outside of it. I am also not the story, because I am left out, or if I am left in, then like a footnote I am relegated to the margins. I am a witness while also being the story's servant and carrier. This is how I might describe myself:

Benin: 1700
Virginia: 1700-1750
Mississippi: 1750-1804
Haiti: 1804-1922
Miami: 1922-1970
Edmonton: 1970-2017
Toronto: 2017-

or

Ghana: 1700
Barbados: 1700-1759
Salem: 1759-1778

Barbados: 1778-1947
Brooklyn: 1948-1979
Barbados: 1979-

or

Songhai: 1700
Saint-Domingue: 1700-1805
Cuba: 1805-1985
Miami: 1985-1990
Dartmouth: 1990-

or

Benin: 1700
Jamaica: 1700-1905
Miami: 1905-1906
New York: 1906-1969
Montréal: 1969-

or

Benin: 1700
Jamaica: 1700-1796
Nova Scotia: 1796-1800
Freetown, Sierra Leone: 1800-

or

Ghana: 1700
Barbados: 1700-1970
Vancouver: 1970-

or

Benin: 1700
Trinidad: 1700-1981
London, England: 1981-1995
Hamilton: 1995-

or

Mali: 1700
Bahia: 1700-1859
Guyana: 1860-1975
Toronto: 1975-

or

Benin: 1700
Pernambuco: 1700-18—
Panama: 18- -18—
St-Vincent: 18— -1919
Chicago: 1919-1924
New York: 1924-1926
Montréal: 1926-

In a list of dates and places, arrivals and departures, we find no individual, although these dates and places contain entire generations. They parenthesize cultures. They suggest bare feet first sinking into the glittering sand of an unfamiliar world. They conjure an awestruck face staring through a lattice of leaves toward a golden waterfall, high in the mythic mountains of El Dorado. They suggest the dawning, or the twilight of a kind of existence. They are the dizzying anxiety of leaving the known world and embarking for the unknown. They are iron and money. They are also like stars whose light continues to travel even after they are extinguished. They are immaterial because they do not dam the flow of people. The anterior dates do not affix beginnings, because the past tumbles backward into darkness, and their future dates do not stop time, because time does not stop, it does not surrender to a number.

Does it matter where or what year I was born? I am in the story, whatever story is being told, but I am not its subject. I am not supposed to have a name because I am the imported help. I am the servant of the story, the still figure someone might mistake for porcelain. There, standing in the corner beneath the palm frond, or there, in the shade of the veranda, invisible and observing, until someone swings a leg up on the plank of a plantation chair, and I remove the boot.

Perhaps I am in the cellar, or at the edge of a field listening, working, and I should quote a poet in whose ear I have whispered, because his words will better explain:

Master of the three paths, you have before you a man who has carried a lot. And truly my friends

I have carried all the way from Elam, from Akkad,
from Sumer... I have carried on my nappy head
that gets along just fine without a little cushion
God, the machine, the road...

There is something of me in Benin, certainly, and yet
I am scattered by the trade, by the trade winds. I am flung
to the southwest, from Île Gorée toward Bahia, then a short
distance north to Pernambuco, up to the Guianas, and then
along that "mighty curve" of the Antilles, from Barbados
to Trinidad and upward through Santo Domingo, Jamaica,
Cuba, up, up through Panama and into Florida, and up
until we reach Mont Royal, then the few short hours north
through snow and spruce to Québec, oldest of walled cities
in North America, and finally across to Halifax, from where
600 Jamaican Maroons weighed anchor for Sierra Leone.

I am populated by other people's lives. In my mind
the lives blur into a vast anonymous sweep of existence, a
movement. The idea that stories are about individuals, that
they have protagonists and antagonists is a simplification
that fuels the market. There exist no central figures. A
person is nobody. No narrator, no voice. A story is a natural
force, like the hurricane, that flings individual names apart.
The Berbice slave rebellion was led by men born in Benin,
some of whom struck for freedom when they were in their
forties and fifties, and who did not surrender to gravity
and the lash, or wilt before the inevitability of torture and
public death. Today, who can draw their likeness? Who
knows the sound of their voices? If in one version they are
heroes, they are criminal rabble in another.

As I make my point, I undermine myself. Why is *I* always the center of the story? I am not I. If any reader attempts to identify I, that single, distinguished letter will widen into a rift, an eternally widening band of darkness and dust.

No beginnings, no end, no characters... what is this but a rambling chronicle with no origin—indeed "too much has been made of origins, all origins are arbitrary"—and no terminus, because every point along the continuum may offer a new origin. The rambling chronicle might begin the year a Haitian teenager runs away from home, which may be the same year a referendum is declared in Québec, one that unleashes an exodus from the province. But does the story begin there, with the parallel flights of the boy and the Anglophones, or does it begin when his parents' plane first touches the runway at the Aéroport International Mirabel in 1986, as they fly from Haiti as an ousted dictator flees into exile and the space shuttle *Challenger* explodes? Or, what if things begin in humbler circumstances on a raft drifting across to Florida, or in a different branch of the grand narrative, earlier, on a vast colonial estate in the coffee producing hills of Xaymaca, reading the Book of Exodus upside-down by firelight, the page swarmed by mosquitoes, or earlier, in the 1700s on a sugar estate in Demerara, or perhaps they begin before that, with a bang—but which bang? The volcanos that shaped the Caribbean islands were echoes of an earlier explosion.

Does the rambling chronicle have to be as dramatic and consequential as an explosion? Instead, can it be words adrift in the timelessness of thought, language and images that stay adrift, or can it just be drift, eternal drift? Can it be a figure standing in the moonlight waiting for a canoe to appear on the river—or perhaps that fragment is too large, too elaborate, too suggestive? Perhaps a person stands in the moonlight by a river, waiting. But why do they have to be waiting for anything? The person may just be standing. They are a person, and that is the only fragment necessary to produce a story. A person who could be anyone. A person whose name or origins we do not know, whose looks are indistinct. A person, adrift. Even that suggests too much of a mystery. A person who isn't anybody of consequence, and who allows the story to depart in all of the directions in which it might depart in real life, which is often irrelevant and inconclusive. And that person who urges the story along, that person is me, and the story never belongs to me, who is nobody and who does not exist.

I try not to emphasize that the story is going anywhere specific. It is simply moving, when it wants to—or is it just the world that is moving, and people are caught in that movement—and my job, as amanuensis, is to allow the world to move through me, to place myself in the story as a porcelain Nubian servant figure, or as a guide in the Amazon, who has no speaking role but who steers the characters through the dream? As they argue and curse in Spanish, dripping with sweat, I lead them through their malarial fever for gold, up to a wall of leaves. They curse and gesticulate, and the wall of leaves morphs into a wall of letters. The letters hover before us, and the Spaniards, confounded, curse that they can't understand. I reach out and push back a sentence, which solidifies into a branch off which fronds hang, and they first hear the roar of a waterfall. I step back, as they peer through the break in the foliage. For a brief moment the world looks upon itself in awe, before the poison arrows fly through the breach. Without that anonymous service there would be no narrative movement. There would be no consciousness. There would be no world.

ACKNOWLEDGEMENTS

I am grateful to those who crossed oceans and continents to establish new homes, to those who were uprooted, to those who marooned, and to those who refused to be erased

To those who sang, played instruments, and shared sound, rhythm, and spirit

To my parents, my brother, my family, and to the late Clarence Roger London

To Melissa-Anne Cobbler, for nurturing the Caribbean cultural connection, and thereby enriching our lives

To Dimitri Nasrallah, Simon Dardick, Nancy Marrelli, and David Drummond at Véhicule Press. A good editor's interest, clean design, and a publisher's investment are essential. They bolster the fortitude a writer needs to solve the narrative conundrums they create for themselves

To David Chariandy, a writer I admire, for the generosity to offer some words of support for this work, and for demonstrating the importance of uplifting other voices

To Nalini Mohabir, H. Nigel Thomas, Tanya Evanson, and Ronald Cummings, who engaged with the work, thought about it, and whose insights into diaspora, migration, and belonging in Canada informed countless editorial decisions

To the festivals and event organizers who have invited me to crisscross the country these past 22 years. Traveling as an artist has broadened my understanding of this country, and has shaped my practice

To Shape&Nature Press in Massachusetts, for publishing an early edition of "Navette", and to Robyn Maynard for referencing "Navette" in her paper, "Reading Black Resistance through Afrofuturism: Notes on post-Apocalyptic Blackness and Black Rebel Cyborgs in Canada," Topia vol. 39

To Hamidou Diop for being the most underdeveloped, yet the most compelling character in Québec fiction

Merci.

ESPLANADE
Books

THE FICTION IMPRINT AT VÉHICULE PRESS

A House by the Sea : A novel by Sikeena Karmali
A Short Journey by Car : Stories by Liam Durcan
Seventeen Tomatoes : Tales from Kashmir : Stories by Jaspreet Singh
Garbage Head : A novel by Christopher Willard
The Rent Collector : A novel by B. Glen Rotchin
Dead Man's Float : A novel by Nicholas Maes
Optique : Stories by Clayton Bailey
Out of Cleveland : Stories by Lolette Kuby
Pardon Our Monsters : Stories by Andrew Hood
Chef : A novel by Jaspreet Singh
Orfeo : A novel by Hans-Jürgen Greif
[Translated from the French by Fred A. Reed]
Anna's Shadow : A novel by David Manicom
Sundre : A novel by Christopher Willard
Animals : A novel by Don LePan
Writing Personals : A novel by Lolette Kuby
Niko : A novel by Dimitri Nasrallah
Stopping for Strangers : Stories by Daniel Griffin
The Love Monster : A novel by Missy Marston
A Message for the Emperor : A novel by Mark Frutkin
New Tab : A novel by Guillaume Morissette
Swing in the House : Stories by Anita Anand
Breathing Lessons : A novel by Andy Sinclair
Ex-Yu : Stories by Josip Novakovich